COUNTERFEIT COWBOY

Ginny Baird

COUNTERFEIT COWBOY
Published by
Winter Wedding Press

Copyright © 2014
Ginny Baird
Trade Paperback
ISBN 978-0-9895892-8-4

Edited by Linda Ingmanson
Cover by Gilded Heart Design

About the Author

From the time that she could talk, romance author Ginny Baird was making up stories, much to the delight—and consternation—of her family and friends. By grade school, she'd turned that inclination into a talent, whereby her teacher allowed her to write and produce plays rather than write boring book reports. Ginny continued writing throughout college, where she contributed articles to her literary campus weekly, then later pursued a career managing international projects with the US State Department.

Ginny has held an assortment of jobs, including school teacher, freelance fashion model, and greeting card writer, and has published more than ten works of fiction and optioned nine screenplays. She has additionally published short stories, nonfiction and poetry, and admits to being a true romantic at heart.

Ginny is the author of several bestselling books, including novellas in her *Holiday Brides Series*. She's a member of Romance Writers of America (RWA), the RWA Published Authors Network (PAN), and Virginia Romance Writers (VRW).

When she's not writing, Ginny enjoys cooking, biking, and spending time with her family in Tidewater, Virginia. She loves hearing from her readers and welcomes visitors to her website http://www.ginnybairdromance.com.

Books by Ginny Baird

Holiday Brides Series
The Christmas Catch
The Holiday Bride
Mistletoe in Maine
Beach Blanket Santa
Baby, Be Mine

Summer Grooms Series
Must-Have Husband
My Lucky Groom
The Wedding Wish
The Get-Away Groom
(Coming Soon!)

A Haunted Holidays Special Edition
The Ghost Next Door
(A Love Story)

Other Titles
Real Romance
The Sometime Bride
Santa Fe Fortune
How to Marry a Matador
Special Delivery
(A Valentine's Short Story)
Counterfeit Cowboy

Bundles
Real Romance and The Sometime Bride
(Gemini Edition)
Santa Fe Fortune and How to Marry a Matador
(Gemini Edition)
The Holiday Brides Collection
(Books 1—4)
A Summer Grooms Selection
(Books 1—3)
Wedding Bells Bundle
(New in 2014!)

Ginny Baird's

COUNTERFEIT COWBOY

When it comes to love,
Only the heart knows for sure…

Chapter One

Eve Parker reached in her closet and yanked out another bridesmaid dress. This was the frilly one with that ridiculous bow on its shoulder. Cornflower blue with a midnight-black velvet skirt. Ugh. Eve tried not to recall how the high waistline of the bodice made her stomach stick out in a pooch at the wedding she'd attended last month.

"Evie!" Aunt Mildred had cried with a mixture of horror and intrigue. "You're not…?" She'd extended a wrinkled hand to cup Eve's belly.

Eve had pushed it away with an embarrassed flush. "Of course not." Then she'd gone to get another glass of champagne and reassure herself. The dress was unflattering, yes. But she hadn't looked *that bad*. Certainly not bad enough for someone to think she was knocked up. Eve paused in her work, reliving the moment…

Eve felt suddenly overheated in the confining fabric of her dress. Even the back of her neck was hot below her mass of fiery red tresses. She'd styled it nicely, and at the bride's instruction had pulled back one side in an enormous barrette. It sported a bow to match the one on her opposite shoulder. Sally said symmetry was everything at weddings. Eve had wondered about that since Sally and her new groom—a yoga instructor from Soho—didn't seem particularly well matched. Or maybe it was the balance that mattered.

A server distributing champagne passed by, and she nabbed one off the tray as she headed in the other direction. She'd step outdoors to cool off. Eve was nearly to the palladium doors when her gaze fell on the buffet table. At the far end, a chef was busily putting together mini shish kebabs stacked with rare roast beef, roasted garlic, and tiny portabella mushrooms. Eve sighed with gratitude, knowing relief was in sight.

She strode toward the man and nabbed one of the narrow shish kebab sticks from where it nested in a box. "Thanks!" she said, smiling brightly. In a lightning-quick move, Eve set her glass on the edge of the table, and twirled up her hair in a French twist spiraling northward from her nape. Next, she took the shish kebab stick and inserted it pointy-end down, securing her pile of hair in place. "Ah," she breathed as the amazed chef stared. "Better."

Then she grabbed her champagne and headed for the patio to clear her head and get some air.

Eve shook off the memory and tossed the offending bridesmaid gown onto her bed with the others. One was teal, another hot pink, a third lemon-drop yellow. She hadn't really gotten mad at Aunt Mildred for implying she was pregnant. After all, Mildred was in her eighties and at the point where she generally said what came to mind. She wasn't even Eve's aunt. She was Sally's. But Eve had known her long enough to understand she was generally an upbeat person. Even if she *did* have the habit of getting into everybody's business. Eve had told Sally she supposed that came with age, but Sally had responded, "No, Aunt Mildred's always been that way."

Eve returned to her closet and pulled out one more dress. This one was dramatic and had actually made her feel beautiful. It was a deep crimson color and made of extra-fine silk. Its silhouette was trim and tasteful, but in Eve's case, ample room had been allowed for the curve of her hips. It had a stylish halter top with a deep dip in front and a flouncy detail ruffle that hit just above the knees. Eve sighed, remembering the lush outdoor wedding that had been held at Fernando Garcia de la Vega's estate in southern Spain.

Two years ago this summer, Eve's best friend, Jessica Bloom, had run off to Spain and married a matador. Ex-matador slash billionaire slash extra-yummy hottie. Plus he was kind and generous and considerate. And he had an accent to die for. *And,* Jess had assured Eve, he was a sex machine.

Eve slumped down on the bed and clutched the dress to her chest. She'd never had that sort of adventure herself. She didn't even believe those whirlwind romances existed until she'd seen one up close with her very own eyes. At first, she'd been worried for her best friend and had tried to talk her out of it. *Really! Leaving your whole life, family, and career behind to start over on some other continent! Is it worth it?*

Once Eve had been around the two of them together, she saw that it was. They'd been head over heels about each other and—two years later—still were. They already had a baby, little Margarita. She was gorgeous too, with her daddy's green eyes and dark hair, but with Jessica's delicate frame.

Shortly after Jess and Fernando had married, they'd tried to fix Eve up with Fernando's best friend. But, as things typically happened for Eve, there was always some complication. Not the least of which was Gustavo's long-lost love, Estrella, coming back into the picture by moving from Barcelona to Seville. It was very tough to compete with Seville when Eve lived in Brooklyn. Besides, her Spanish was atrocious. Who on earth was she kidding?

Eve gently laid the silk dress on top of the pile, smoothing it out. "Always a bridesmaid," she mused with a sad smile. At least she had her work to keep her happy. *Lie alert!* She wasn't happy so much as busy. Yeah, but busy was good. Right? The only trouble was that she didn't feel challenged enough. Nine months ago, she'd left her job in copyediting at a midsize publisher to join the editorial department of the hip women's magazine, *Make It Count.* The motto of the rag was *No time to waste, girlfriend!* It was targeted to women in their twenties and thirties, and each issue brimmed with advice on how to work better, live better, and love better. Plus, there were always features on some major star who was really *making it count.* You know, those terribly annoying celebrities who seemed to have it all, do it all, and look perfectly coiffed while they were at it. Even in sweatpants. Forget that they had personal trainers and chefs to trim their figures, accountants to do their books, and managers to get them their next gig.

Eve waved it all aside with a flip of her wrist. *Who wants all that, anyway?* She didn't. All Eve aspired to was a simple life. A simple, happy life. If she could manage to keep a boyfriend, that would be nice too. But for whatever reason, she hadn't been able to. She'd been accused of being too brainy, too serious, or too intrusive. Seriously? Just because she wanted to know things? Curiosity was the mark of a good mind. Everybody knew that. Plus, her eighth-grade teacher had said so, and Eve still trusted that advice to this day. Besides, she actually preferred the word inquisitive. That really fit much better and didn't carry such a negative connotation.

Her dad had always encouraged Eve to play to her strengths, and wanting to know things was one of them. This was precisely why she was going to ask her boss for a promotion. It felt like she'd been copyediting forever, and doing it at the magazine seemed particularly tiresome. At least at the publisher's, she'd been able to get into the meat of a story or some nonfiction idea she'd never thought of before. It was interesting and revealing to study a whole book and check for any glitches.

When you're reading three hundred and fifty words, there aren't many challenges to be found. Everything was fairly straightforward—and in present tense. *You know you want that new look, so now's the time to go and get it! Read* Make It Count's *top-ten list for getting your glam on this year!* Eve cringed, knowing it wasn't great literature, but hey, it paid the bills. She didn't write the copy anyhow. She just caught the mistakes. And even in something that simple, she found them. It originally read *newt* instead of *new*, and *glam* had somehow morphed into *clam.* Good thing she knew the lingo and could translate.

But Eve was tired of catching other people's errors. She wanted to charge out there and commit a few of her own! Or at least make a go of it. Being a reporter, that was. She believed she had talent and possessed the right skill set. All she had to do was get her boss to agree. *Make It Count* didn't have too many regular positions, because they most often used freelancers.

Still, everyone knew the division's current assistant, Winnipeg Marshall, was on her way out. Winnie'd been picked up by a large newspaper in south Florida to do some serious work. She'd be covering immigration and health issues and couldn't wait to get away from the cold so she could stretch out by the pool in her bikini. She'd gotten the job on account of her uncle's brother-in-law or some weird family connection like that. The men had been pontooning, and one happened to mention to the other they could use somebody new and sharp at the paper. Winnie's uncle—or in-law, Eve couldn't remember which—had said, *"What a coincidence! I just happen to know a really great writer in New York City!"*

Winnie had been squealing with joy to her compatriots ever since. The only ones who didn't know she was leaving yet were her direct supervisor and their editorial director, Ross. She planned to tell them both at the end of this week. This could leave an opening for Eve. She hoped, she hoped, she *hoped*. Eve crossed her fingers and laid her hand in her lap. Something had to go right for her this year. Her *Make It Count* annual horoscope forecast had said so. It had even gone so far as to suggest—*ha-ha*—that this was the year Eve would meet the man of her dreams. Seeing as how it was already summer, her prospects didn't look good.

Chapter Two

Eve sat at her desk, eyes fixed on her computer screen. She had her hand in a bag of Milky Milanos and was just about to dig out another cookie when Glenn approached.

"Chief wants you." Glenn was always quite glib and pulled together. He was the only man on the job who regularly wore a suit besides their editor in chief, Ross. Perhaps he aspired to be Ross one day. In that case, he'd have to work on the hair.

Glenn tucked an errant strand of dark hair behind his ear. It fell just to his chin and was parted in the middle, which always made him look like he worked too hard. Like an overly eager schoolboy who was…now adjusting his glasses frames and staring straight at Eve. She realized she'd paused midair with the cookie hovering in her hand halfway to her mouth. She glanced at the cookie, then quickly tucked it back in its bag as if she'd never intended to eat it.

"What's Ross want with me?" she asked, dropping the cookie bag into her desk drawer and sliding it shut.

Glenn watched with mild amusement. "Were those peanut butter chocolates in there?"

"No."

"Peppermint patties too?"

"Look, Glenn, it's been a rough week."

"It's only Monday."

"Weekend, I mean." She blew a hard breath. "The weekend was tough."

Glenn's brow rose, questioning. She didn't need to tell him she'd had another disaster date on Saturday and had spent all day Sunday clearing her closet of bridesmaid dresses to cart off to charity.

"None of your business."

He gave an exaggerated sigh and eyed his watch. It was very retro to wear one, and Glenn's looked like the expensive kind.

"Right." Eve stood and smoothed her skirt. She glanced at Glenn, a thought occurring. Winnie wasn't supposed to give notice until Friday. Could she possibly have spilled early? Everyone in the office knew Eve had been hoping for Winnie's job. Everyone but Winnie, that was. Perhaps she was oblivious or, more to the point, maybe she didn't care. "You don't think it's about the promotion?"

"No way to know until you go in there."

"Wish me luck," Eve whispered.

"Luck," he said in a pert little way. Eve didn't know how he could be so annoying, but he was. Even when he was attempting to be nice. Without warning, Glenn reached toward her and plucked something hard from the back of her hair. "Best to go in without the pencil," he said, handing it to her.

Eve's curls spilled to her shoulders, and she ran her fingers through them to smooth them. That was one habit Ross had complained about: the fact that Eve sometimes stuck odd objects in her hair. He said it looked unprofessional. Especially after Eve had ordered takeout Chinese. It wasn't like it was really her fault. She didn't do it consciously. Sometimes the back of her neck felt hot.

She shot Glenn a timid smile and laid the pencil on her desk. "Thanks."

Before she turned to leave, Glenn surprised her with a thought. "I hope you get it, Eve." His brown eyes were sincere.

"What?"

"You know what." He lowered his voice a notch. "Winnie's position."

She tried not to squeal. "Ross knows?"

Glenn nodded. "I think you're the right one for the job."

Eve beamed brightly, feeling her confidence surge. "I *know* I am."

When Eve entered Ross's office, he was peering outside at the window cleaners who were hoisting themselves up on their platform from the floor below. It was a fairly precarious job, particularly since they were on the eighteenth floor. Eve waited for him to notice her, but he didn't, so she subtly cleared her throat.

Ross pivoted toward her with a broad smile. "Eve! Welcome, welcome. Do come in!" His shock of black hair towered high at the crown, sweeping in elegant form from either temple. It was an oddly feminine style, offset by a pencil-thin, wraparound beard and moustache. White teeth gleamed down at her, but Eve knew better than to be impressed by dental hygiene. She'd guessed he'd had them capped years before.

"You wanted to see me?"

"Yes." He stepped behind her and shut the door. He motioned for her to sit, then dropped into his black leather chair behind his Lucite desk. Beyond him, two window cleaners leveled themselves against the building, then took to furiously swabbing the glass.

One of the workers seemed to peer over Ross's shoulder and gaze straight in Eve's direction. For the life of her, it looked like he was wiggling his eyebrows! Was it Eve's imagination, or was he making eyes at her?

This was just her luck. When she was in a roomful of professionals, she could scarcely get a man to notice her. Now, here was some workman openly ogling her through the glass!

Eve primly crossed her legs and tried to ignore it.

Ross caught something in her stance and glanced over his shoulder. "Oh, for crying out loud!"

The workman's face creased in a grin as he shot a wink at Ross. Ross blinked and shook his head. "It's Carlton!"

"Who's Carlton?" Eve asked with surprise.

Ross grabbed the cord to the blinds and dropped them down hard. He swiveled his chair back toward Eve. "He used to deliver my paper. I think he's stalking me, actually."

"Is he...?"

"Interested? Probably. Not that I'd be interested back." Ross held up his hand and flashed Eve his wedding band. "Wife and two kids at home."

Ross lifted the phone from the console on his desk. "If you'll excuse me." Then he put in a call to security to complain about the window cleaner.

"Now!" he said, finally returning his attention to her. "Where were we?"

With all the window-cleaning excitement, Eve had nearly lost track. "Um... Glenn said—"

Ross snapped his fingers, remembering. "That's right! Reporting. It might interest you to know a new position's opened up."

"Really?" Eve asked, feigning surprise. "Where?"

"Jackie's assistant. What's her name?" His fingers drummed the desk.

"Winnie."

"Yes, Winnie. Anyway, it appears she's moving away. Florida, of all places! In the dead of summer. Some folks you just can't figure."

Eve didn't find the temperatures in New York particularly moderate in July, but decided not to say so to Ross. "So…" she began tentatively. "You're looking to fill her position?"

"Only temporarily."

Eve's face sagged with disappointment.

"The fact is, we will be filling her slot eventually. On a permanent basis, I mean. Just not yet. We'll need Jackie back here to interview and help select a candidate." Jackie, the senior reporter in the division, was out on maternity leave. Prior to taking time off, she'd worked hard to get extra articles in and leave things for production with Winnie. Eve supposed that was what Ross wanted help with now. More paper shuffling. Moving pieces from one department to the next. That sounded even more mundane than copyediting. At least she had experience with that.

She thought she knew the answer, but opted to ask anyway. "So, there will be no new reporting while Jackie's away?"

"Oh, I didn't say that." Ross lifted a manila file folder from his desk and passed it to Eve.

She flipped it open, not understanding. It was a printout of some Internet article. She met Ross's gaze. "Wild West Brides?"

"Can you imagine? And I thought the days of the mail-order bride were *long gone*."

Eve studied the article again, where the copy read "Come away to the Wild, Wild West and Meet the Cowboy of Your Dreams! Fun Dates and Adventure!" There was a little asterisk there, and she followed it to the bottom of the page to read the fine print. "Promises of proposals not guaranteed." Why, this wasn't an article at all! It was an advertisement. "It doesn't sound like mail-order. Ross, this is a dating service!"

"And people are taking him up on it."

"Who?"

Ross motioned for her to flip through the file, and she did until she found it: a clip from a small-town newspaper article on rugged Wyoming bachelor Ted Walker. He was broad-chested and handsome in a cowboy hat, flannel shirt, and jeans. Worn leather boots hitched into the stirrups of the huge quarter horse he mounted as he sat up straight in the saddle, his warm, confident smile dazzling. Eve sighed involuntarily. "Wow."

"I know, right?" Ross teased. "The window cleaner should be winking at him."

Eve laughed. "I still don't get what this is all about."

"It's something Jackie was working on. I was going to send her out this summer. But then the baby thing came up..."

Eve's heart pumped harder. "You're not waiting until she gets back?"

"Here's the deal." Ross leaned forward with a confidential whisper. "That other magazine in town, *Real Women Today*, they're working on a similar story: 'Best Bachelors of the West.'"

"You're thinking we can scoop them?"

"I don't even think they know about 'Wild West Brides.' But if they start digging around for their issue, they're going to find him."

"Ted."

"That's right."

Eve gazed at him, understanding. "You don't want *them* to scoop us."

"Not when this is *our* story. We found it first. Which is why we're rushing it to print. Eve," he said with a pinched, tight smile, "I'm sending you to Wyoming!"

Eve swallowed hard, her face flushed. "Me?"

"I trust you can write." He pulled her résumé from a stack of papers on his desk. "You graduated with honors in English."

"Yes, but—"

"*And,* you've put in time copyediting, which means you'll do due diligence. We can count on you to be thorough."

"But, Ross—"

"Plus," he said even more brightly, "you're the only one on staff who rides horses!"

This hit Eve out of left field. "What? No!"

"Glenn told me. You had that Spanish thing going on. Or should I say *fling*? No matter, as your boss, I really can't comment. I heard it was with a matador or something. Someone who owned a horse ranch."

"Actually, it was a winery, and that was my friend—"

"Eve," he said, stopping her cold. "Did you or did you not spend six weeks last summer on a horse ranch in Spain?"

"It was a vineyard," she said weakly.

"Aha!" Ross raised an index finger. "There were horses there, weren't there? Very fine ones. Spanish stallions?"

"There were horses, sure—"

"See now!" He stood to indicate their meeting was closing. "You're perfect for the job. You're young, single…female. And! You can ride a horse!"

"Ross."

"I'll have Glenn make your travel arrangements."

He reached across the desk and shook her hand. "Welcome to cub reporting. Meet with Glenn in the morning. He'll tell you everything you need to know."

Eve stood and inched toward the door, her knees shaking. Sure, she wanted to take more on, but not all this! She'd only been on a horse once! And she'd been thrown off! *Wyoming?* She was going to Wyoming? She didn't know a thing about it, other than that there were cowboys there. Apparently one of them was called Ted Walker. The back of her neck felt hot. Eve fought the urge to twist up her hair.

Ross's gaze followed her. "You do this right, there could be good things in store."

Chapter Three

On the far side of Jackson Hole, Ted Walker strode purposefully toward the barn, leading two horses. His buddy Brian trailed behind him, reining in two mavericks of his own. They were on Sunnyvale Ranch, a bright spot in a valley snuggled up against the Grand Teton Mountains. Even in summer, the range was capped with snow. Winds roiled across the field, threatening to unseat Ted's hat. With the sun going down, the air was getting frisky. He tapped his hat down on his head to secure it. "I think today went well," he told Brian.

"Better than well. It seems we made another major score." He followed Ted into the barn, then corrected himself. "*Scores.*"

It was true. The three couples they'd set up all seemed to be getting along great with one another. And each day's activities brought them closer. If all went well with the rest of the week, by this time on Saturday he and Brian would be hearing wedding bells, or at least news of some impending engagements. Wild West Brides had been an enormous success. While proposals weren't guaranteed, when you put men and women together who were bent on marriage, there wasn't a whole lot more to do. Introduce them in a pretty locale, send them off on some exciting adventures, expose big-city females to the allure of the wild Wild West. Let nature and romance take its course.

Most of the women weren't shrinking violets either, or damsels in distress. They were bright professional women with accomplished careers, and they wanted just one last thing: a man of their own. They came from all over the country and didn't worry a lick about relocating. If they found the right guy, they knew that somehow the two of them would work it out. Maybe he'd move there, or she'd come here. It all boiled down to four little letters, ones they couldn't buy in shares in the stock market: L. O. V. E.

These women weren't crazy to think they could find that through Wild West Brides. The testimonials were outstanding, and many came through referrals from their friends. Brian's computerized matchmaking program helped set up the most likely matches, then the moon and the mountain air did the rest.

The local boys sure had been happy about it. Even to this day, the male population was more than double the number of females. In the eighteen months since it had opened, Wild West Brides had become a booming business. And their reputation was spreading by word of mouth. Bachelors came here to participate from all over the state. A few had even come from Idaho and Montana. Ted and Brian had made a mint in the process.

"Yep," Ted answered as they put the horses up for the night. "Another good day. I'm still thanking my lucky stars you wrote that computer program."

"And I'm still thanking mine you knew a thing or two about running a ranch." Brian elbowed him with an exaggerated edge and winked. *"Partner."*

Ted chuckled good-naturedly and patted his back. "Pays to read books."

Eve looked up from the loaded e-reader in her hand. "What's this?"

Glenn leaned against the wall beside her desk. "Thought you might enjoy a little airline reading."

"Ten Tips for Turning His Head. Riding Lessons for the Inexperienced Horsewoman. Acting Basics?"

"Well, you do have a role to play," Glenn said matter-of-factly.

Eve eyed Glenn suspiciously. "What are you talking about?"

She placed the e-reader on her desk beside the stack of other stuff Glenn had brought her. Proof of purchase for her e-ticket, the hotel reservation confirmation… A great big, glossy trifold leaflet from Wild West Brides. The women were seated on horseback, with outrageously handsome men positioned behind them. Though their outfits varied from the traditional to funky punk, each female dressed as a bride. This notwithstanding, the guys were still all dressed like cowboys.

"It's a fantasy thing, I'd guess," Glenn said, noting her eye on the photo.

"I can't believe he really does it." She met Glenn's gaze. "I mean, actually is successful."

"The statistics are printed on the back."

"Yeah, but… Who? I mean, ha-ha…" Suddenly, Eve had a vision of riding off into the sunset with the undeniably hot and rugged Ted Walker. Their horse cantered faster and faster, as they dodged rolling tumbleweeds and desert cacti. His chest was solid and muscled, his six-pack taut as she wound her arms around him, clinging tightly—her front pressed to his back, the breeze raking her hair. She removed the chopstick from her twist and let her locks fly wild. Wild in the untamed wind!

"Eve!"

"Huh?" She turned to find Glenn staring at her. Without even realizing it, she'd pulled the pencil from her piled-up hair and now clenched it in her teeth. She removed it from her mouth and hastily dropped it into her pencil holder.

"Where were you just now?"

"I was just...um." Her gaze flitted to the brochure, and she slid it under the e-reader. "Mentally going over my schedule." She shook out her hair and gazed at him. "I'm sorry, what was it you were saying about Ross? Wasn't he going to supply a list of questions?"

"Questions?"

"For the interview."

Glenn hedged. "It's not exactly going to be that kind of interview."

"What kind?"

"The kind you're thinking of."

"How do you know what I'm thinking of?"

"I generally do."

She glanced at the pencil in her cup and felt hot all over.

"Are you feeling all right?"

"Yes. Yes." She met his eyes. "Just what are you getting at, Glenn? That I'm supposed to ad-lib it?"

His face brightened. "Yes! That's it. Just go with the flow, sort of. Once you get one piece of information, dig for the next."

"O...kay. I'll be sure to take good notes."

"Oh no, you can't do that."

"No notes? Why not?"

"Could throw things off."

"I'll record it, then, to play back later when—"

Glenn solemnly shook his head.

Eve blinked hard. Something about this wasn't adding up. "I might be good, but I'm not *that* good. I'm new at this. It's best I write some things down in case I forget."

"Use your cell phone, then. Like a camera. Record every Kodak moment."

Eve rubbed the back of her neck, which was steaming. "I thought I was supposed to learn about Wild West Brides?"

"You are!"

"Meaning, interview Ted Walker."

"Not for this feature. Ross wants a much more personal angle than that."

Uh-oh. Eve felt an ambush coming. "How personal?"

Glenn stepped toward her and lowered his voice. "Eve, you're not just going to write about Wild West Brides. You're supposed to be one!"

"Be one?" Her voice squeaked, and Eve cupped her mouth. "What on earth do you mean?"

"Just that. I've booked you the Buffalo Bill Package. It's a five-day adventure."

"You're kidding."

"Seven days, including travel."

Panic struck her. "This is where the horse thing came from...? Glenn! Why did you lie?"

"I didn't lie to Ross. I embellished."

"You told him I rode horses!"

"Haven't you? Ever?"

"Just once, when I was twelve. My friend and I found a pony tied to a tree in the country and tried to get on it. It threw us both off!"

"What about that thing in Spain? Your...whatever you want to call it...with the matador?"

"It wasn't me with the matador! It was Jess!"

"Who's Jess?"

"Only my best friend since... Oh, never mind."

Eve dropped her face in her hands, and waves of curly hair spilled forward, draping her shoulders.

Glenn spoke softly now, consoling. "I was only trying to help, you know."

She stared up at him, her head spinning.

"I know how badly you wanted that position. Winnie's job."

"I don't believe Winnie was ever slated to become a Wild West Bride!"

"No." He cocked his head to the side. "She was never that lucky."

Eve wondered how hard it could be. "I don't have to pretend to be a cowgirl?"

"Not necessary. Most of the women who sign up for this program are city girls."

Eve blew a small breath, partially consoled. "Well, good." After a beat, she studied Glenn's face for clues. "How come Ross didn't tell me this himself?"

"He knows we're friends." Eve had never considered this. Not that she was opposed to a friendship. It was more like she'd always viewed Glenn as a little stuffy. But maybe he wasn't all bad. Here he was, trying to help her! Or perhaps he was just trying to win points with Ross. "He thought you'd take it better coming from me."

She met his eyes with a challenge. "So, how am I supposed to get out of it, then? Get out of the little charade once it's done?"

"No problem! It says right there in the fine print, *proposals not guaranteed.* Doesn't matter who you're set up with. Just say it didn't work out."

"I'm supposed to give the *it's not you, it's me* speech?"

"You'll think of something. Whatever comes naturally. Meanwhile"—he patted her back with a smile—"just imagine all the great intel you'll pick up. You're going to see that Brides operation from the inside out, and I'll bet whatever you learn will be enlightening to—oh…"—he grinned—"about twenty million readers."

"I don't like the thought of hurting somebody's feelings."

"Then don't. Be upfront with the guy you're paired with. Say you're not in it for the long haul. Just experimenting. Looking to make friends. Say your sister put you up to it. Something like that."

"I'll say I was put up to it, all right," Eve muttered under her breath.

"What's that?"

The truth was, the assignment did sound a tiny bit exciting. Flying out to Wyoming to meet some real-life cowboys. She'd never seen any except in the movies, and had certainly never met any up close. Eve wondered if they really called their cattle dogies and said things like giddyup. And Glenn was right about being honest. At least regarding her intentions, or lack thereof. She wouldn't have to hurt anyone's feelings, and when all was said and done, the owner of the business, Ted Walker, was likely to thank her. Just think of all the positive publicity her piece could bring to Wild West Brides.

"All right," Eve said, deciding with sudden certainty. "I'll do it."

"I thought you'd come around." Glenn grinned. "And, hey, you might even find yourself your very own cowboy."

Oh, sure she would. And, by this time next month, she'd be dressed all in white, instead of in one of the many colors that had been in her closet. "Ha-ha," Eve said with a smirk.

Chapter Four

Ten days later, Eve found herself on the back of a horse. She could never have gotten on without the help of that handsome cowboy. She thought he'd said his name was Brian. It was hard to remember with the sun bearing down on her and causing sweat to dribble down her cleavage. While her outfit said *Western*, at the moment she didn't find it practical. Her plaid ladies' blouse was cuffed at the sleeves and tucked neatly into the waistband of her jeans, only making them fit more tightly. She didn't have an inch to spare at her waistline. Okay, okay. Quarter of an inch, fraction of one…

Eve took in the other women in a casual way and waved. The one with a long dark braid flung forward over her shoulder seemed approachable. The woman with short blonde hair did not. As if to bear out her instincts, the brunette smiled. It was a warm smile, relaxed and friendly. But the blonde's grin was tightly pinched. It looked like someone had pasted it on against her will. Maybe she didn't want to be here either. Eve leaned toward her with sympathy. "Sister put you up to it, huh?"

She cocked her chin with surprise, her perfectly layered hair bouncing. "What?"

"Everybody got that?" Brian glanced around the group and stared straight at Eve. She adjusted her sunglasses in a panic. No, she hadn't heard a word! Luckily, he repeated, "If you drop your reins, don't reach for them. Just call to Ted up front, and he'll come help you."

That reminded her. Where precisely *was* Ted Walker, anyway? Wasn't he supposed to run this little rodeo? And what about the men? Shouldn't there be three of them for the three women here? As if in answer to her question, four men on horseback rounded the barn. The other women sat up at attention. It occurred to Eve that Brian was the only guy who wasn't riding. "Where's your horse?" she asked him.

"My…?" He chuckled in understanding, seemingly flattered she'd wanted him along. "Staying home on the range, little lady. Someone's got to rule the roost."

More like man the phones, Eve thought. She glanced back at the rustic building that served as Wild West Brides' center of operations. It was the intake center where they'd all signed their liability waivers and had received initial instructions about the week. There was the trail ride today, a Wild West safari tomorrow… And who knew what came next? It was hard enough to keep up with the itinerary for the next forty-eight hours. They were all staying in the same hotel and would have a meet-up cocktail hour later this afternoon. The trail ride was just a fun way to break the ice.

For meals and so on, they were mostly on their own. That was when they were supposed to pair up as couples, Eve supposed, and grab more private time getting to know one another. She'd seen on her paperwork that she and a cowboy named Scott had dinner reservations for tomorrow at eight. There were no last names used here, only first ones. That was in the contract she'd signed. This way, all were free to have a good time without feeling undue pressure about things going forward. Eve had shaken her head, reading this last part. Pressure? No pressure at all when one signed on for Wild West Brides! Of course there was pressure. Heaps of it. People didn't merely register for a week of fun. They were hoping to meet their lifetime partners.

The leader of the approaching pack of horses tipped his hat in the women's direction with a cordial smile. She recognized his face at once. He was even more stunning in person. When he spoke, he practically oozed masculinity in that rugged cowboy way. "Howdy, ladies. Welcome to your first Wild West Brides adventure!" A vision of herself riding behind him flashed through Eve's mind, and her skin burned even hotter than it already was. Her face must have been sweating, because her sunglasses started to dip forward. She flipped them up on her head, settling them temporarily on her crown so she could drag a sleeve across her dripping forehead.

"I'm sorry," Ted said. "I know it's hotter than blazes out here in the sun. Once we get on the trail, it won't be so bad." He glanced around the group, speaking to both the men and the women. "There are water bottles in your saddle bags if you need them."

Eve gratefully reached behind her. Her mouth was as parched as dirt. She needed a drink right now.

"Just be careful when you're reaching ba—"

The moment he said it, Eve felt her rear start to slide. Even that was on fire in this saddle! "Ahhhh!" She desperately clung to the saddle horn with one hand as she clutched the water bottle with another. Her body was contorted all sideways, like some sort of weird gymnast doing a midair pirouette. Only she wasn't in the air—yet!

Her horse whinnied with agitation and stomped its hoof on the earth. What was that horrible sound like a woman screeching at the top of her lungs? It only made the horse madder. It started to dance around and around in circles, and the water bottle crashed to the ground, its cap popping open and water bubbling out everywhere. Eve's head spun as she flailed her free arm wildly, trying to get a grip on the saddle, and she dug her knees into the horse.

The horse bounced her up and down, up and down, trying to shake her off like an annoying, human-size dragonfly. Eve felt like a lady in a circus, only she wasn't trained for this!

This was it. She was going to die. And on her very first day in Wyoming! First full day. Everyone knew travel days didn't count. Just then, she heard the *kaboom-kaboom* of thunder. That was her heart! Careening out of control! She could see the obit now: *Eve Parker, reporter. Dead at age thirty-one from cardiac arrest.* She'd better get the reporter credit if she had to die for it!

Just as she was about to tip out of the saddle, a denim-clad leg appeared beside her, and her horse whinnied to a halt. Eve stared down the leg toward the boot in the stirrup, then all the way back up into his eyes. Ted Walker gazed down at her with worry. "Are you all right?" He held her by the shoulder closest to the ground, bracing her so she wouldn't slide from the saddle completely. Eve wondered briefly if that was the horse exhaling in maniacal sputters—or if it was her.

With tender skill, Ted eased her back up into her saddle until she sat upright. Brian stood before her horse, holding her reins as the others just gawked, slack-jawed. Eve's face flamed. Her words came out on puffs of air, her heart still hammering. "Um, yeah. Sorry!"

Ted shot Brian a look. "Maybe we should can the trail ride for today?"

The others started to mutter their protests as their faces fell with disappointment.

Ted authoritatively raised his hand. "Not for everyone. I meant for Eve."

"I'll stay back too," one of the men offered gallantly. He had a square jaw and kind brown eyes. "It wouldn't do for her to wait all alone."

"Thanks, Scott," Brian answered. "But she won't be alone. I'll be here."

"All right, then," Ted said to Brian. "Why don't you *gently* lead her horse back to the barn and—"

It struck Eve that they were deciding her fate for her. "Wait a minute! Don't I get a say in this?"

Ted adjusted his hat and studied her face. "Beg pardon?"

"What if I don't want to go back to the barn?" Eve was a little embarrassed she came off sounding more like a spoiled child than a confident woman. She gathered herself and tried to exude a more dignified air. She couldn't flub up the assignment on her very first try. That would be awful. How would she explain it to Ross? "What I mean is, I would still very much like to go on the trail ride. I don't see why I shouldn't."

The blonde just shook her head, while Scott stroked his chin with amusement. None of the others said a word. All eyes were on Ted. This was his call.

"Are you sure, missy?" he asked in his deep cowboy twang. "I wouldn't want you to do anything you're not comfortable with."

Eve squinted up at him in the sunlight. "I'm plenty comfortable, thank you." She reached for her sunglasses but realized they'd flown off her head.

"Brian," Ted said, "can you grab an extra pair of ladies' shades from the checkout?"

"Oh no, really," Eve started. "Don't trouble your—"

"No trouble." He grinned, and her head went all woozy. Maybe the sun was getting to her again. "We want everyone well equipped for this adventure."

Eve figured she could tough it out with, or without, the glasses. They probably wouldn't be gone long anyway. Still, she appreciated the gesture. Ted Walker was shaping up to be a considerate man. Or perhaps that was just part of his business persona. Eve was grateful either way. "Thanks, Ted."

"Want more water for the ride?"

She stared at the ground where the horse had trampled her plastic water bottle with its prancing hooves. *Oh! There are my sunglasses. Smashed to smithereens as well.*

"How long is it?" she asked, not wanting to trouble him further.

"Two hours. Maybe a tad more."

"Two *hours*?" Her voice rose in a squeak.

Ted whistled to Brian, who was halfway to the welcome center, and made a drinking motion with his hand. Brian gave him a thumbs-up, indicating he got it.

Ted locked on Eve's gaze. "Not changing your mind?"

"Not a chance."

Dark eyes danced. "Good."

Brian returned momentarily and handed Eve a bottle of water and some sunglasses. She slipped on the shades and took a long swig of water before recapping the bottle and very carefully sliding it into her saddlebag.

"Better?" Ted asked.

Eve nodded, still embarrassed. Scott sidled up beside her, offering his companionship and compassion. "I'm glad that you're okay," he told her. "And extra glad you're coming along."

Ted took the two of them in, clearly satisfied the day was improving, then pivoted his horse around. The other horses and riders were growing impatient. It was time to get this show on the road.

"Ready to put a little hitch in your giddy-up?"

Enthusiastic whistles and hollers greeted him.

"Then, ladies and gents, single file after me! Gayle," he said to the brunette, "you line up first, and Stephen can follow. "Then Danni," he said, indicating the blonde, "and Chet, Scott, and Eve."

Eve realized with sudden horror this placed her last! *What if I'm left behind? What if I'm lost in the brush!* Her eyes flitted to the high ridge of the mountains abutting the valley. *What if I fall off a cliff?* "I don't want to be last!" she said, her voice rising.

Brian already had been helping the others get into position just as Ted had ordered. He cast a questioning gaze at Ted. "She has a point," Ted answered. "Better not put her last."

"I'll bring up the rear," Scott answered. He seemed to have command of his horse, as if he'd done this before. "Don't worry," he whispered to Eve as he passed her. "I've got your back."

Chapter Five

Ted sat easily in his saddle, letting Tex lead the way. He didn't have to show his steed which way to go. The big quarter horse had been up and down this trail facing the Teton Range many times. As they cut through the trees, the incline before them steepened, opening up to a rocky ledge that wound its way around this smaller mountain. When they got to the top, they'd be afforded a magnificent view of both the Grand Tetons and the valley below, which housed his Sunnyvale Ranch.

He heard voices behind him and knew his guests were chatting easily. He and Brian had taken care with these matches, as usual. This bonding experience on the trail would provide an exciting early memory upon which each couple could build. He'd see how it played out this evening over drinks.

Ted could generally tell by the end of the first day how well the couples were meshing. The happy fact was, all of his and Brian's matches had worked splendidly so far. A few of the relationships had taken a little longer than others to get going. But each of them had panned out in the end. He and Brian kept waiting for the other shoe to drop. He figured that, one of these days, and simply due to human nature, one of their matches wouldn't make it. Each time Ted led a new adventure, he secretly hoped today wouldn't be that day.

Stephen and Gayle seemed to be getting along already. It was a little too early to tell about Danni and Chet, but it appeared those two held promise as well. But the redhead? Whoa, Nelly. Ted couldn't help but feel the tiniest bit guilty for pairing her with Scott. She might have seemed the perfect match for him on paper. But in person? Man, that filly was a mess!

Ted peered over his shoulder for maybe the tenth time in the last twenty minutes to glance at Eve. Yep, she was still on her horse and clinging on tight as if her life depended on it. Waves of curly red hair spilled past her shoulders and bounced as her horse headed sure-footedly up the trail. She was trying to be polite and answer Scott's questions, but Ted could tell most of her attention was focused on the trek ahead.

They rounded a bend, and she seemed to pale as she viewed the incline before her. Fear worried her big brown eyes, and Ted had the crazy notion he should be back there by her side, gently taking the reins of her horse in his hands and sliding up into her saddle to lead her. She had a fine, womanly figure, in snug-fitting jeans and a form-clinging flannel shirt that was honestly too warm for Wyoming in summer. Ted could nearly envision her arms around him, her soft and curvaceous body pressed to his back. *Whoa there, cowboy!* Ted shifted in his saddle, realizing he was letting his imagination get the best of him, and that imagination was talking to his body in a most inappropriate way.

What was wrong with him today? He'd never been turned on by one of his guests before. All *brides* were strictly off limits, and he knew it. He wasn't interested in finding someone for himself, anyway. Ever since Rebecca, it had been all he could do to focus on his work. And working to deliver happy unions to others was the perfect solution for Ted's ravaged heart. There was no time to sit around and mope when he had serious matchmaking to do.

"Ted?" a woman called tentatively. He glanced over his shoulder to find Danni pointing near the back of their line. It was Eve again, and Scott was backing up his horse to try to assist her. "Hang on there, partner!" he cautioned the other man. "Not so fast on this hill! The path is narrow. Your horse might slip."

"I thought you said they were sure-footed?" Gayle asked with worry.

"They are." Ted easily dismounted, then looped his reins around the narrow trunk of a tree. "Just not when walking backward and doubled-up. This trail is meant for one horse at a time." He slipped past the others and worked his way back to Eve.

She shrugged apologetically. "I'll try to hang on better next time. I was reaching for my sunglasses in my shirt pocket and—"

Ted handed her the reins. "Best to keep both hands on the saddle horn for the next little bit. You can wrap the reins around them like this."

Eve watched his expert moves, then latched on tight. "Going to get steeper?"

"Oh yeah."

Brown eyes locked on his, and Ted's heart rate whipped into a canter. He had to stop this. Stop this right now. "You'll do fine," he said in an even tone he hoped sounded reassuring. He wanted to let Eve know that he was in charge. That no harm would come to her on his watch. "I haven't lost a Wild West bride yet."

Ted, grinned, and Eve's heart fluttered. Wait, no! This was all wrong. That wasn't attraction talking; it was fear. Fear that made her pulse race into overdrive.

Eve's temperature spiked. She didn't dare try to twist her hair up now. Ted was already halfway back to his horse when she called to him. "How much steeper?" she asked, afraid of the answer.

Ted pointed to a ridge on the far side of the valley. It looked like one of those precipitous overlooks cowboys used to perch on while scouring for stagecoach robbers or scouting for Indians. "See that ledge over yonder? That's where we're headed."

"Cool," Gayle said.

"Way cool," Chet added.

But Eve just squealed. "*What?*"

Scott chuckled behind her. "It's all right. Just trust your horse."

It wasn't Eve's horse that she doubted. It was her own ability to stay in her saddle. That would be tough to do if she completely passed out. They began moving again, and Eve felt herself growing light-headed. She realized with horror that her life was in this animal's hands. And they hadn't exactly gotten off to a great start. Best to change all that now, while there was time. She spoke softly in soothing tones, whispering so the others wouldn't hear her.

"You're a good horse. Such a good horse. You can do this."

He seemed to know the way as he carried her higher, scrambling up over rocky terrain toward the deep blue sky. The sun sank lower and wasn't nearly as blinding. Eve took in the mountains beyond them, astounded by their beauty. The Grand Tetons were enormous and rugged, and covered with snow at their highest peeks. They almost reminded her of pictures she'd seen of the Swiss Alps, though she'd never been there.

Eve felt dizzy again and wondered if the altitude was bothering her. It wouldn't do to faint dead away now. She might tumble off this very mountain! She averted her gaze from the precipitous drop to her right, not even wanting to think about what was at the bottom—or how far down that might be. Eve tightened her thighs around her horse, hugging firmly with her calves and knees. As terrified as she was, Eve had to see this ride through to the end.

She'd barely even spoken with Ted and still had everything to ask him about Wild West Brides. Perhaps tonight at the cocktail hour, once this harrowing adventure was done, she'd have more of an opportunity. She set her gaze ahead on the trail to where Ted led their group. He moved surely in his saddle like he hadn't a care in the world. But of course, he'd done this trip a million times. Plus, he was a real cowboy. A man born and bred in the West.

"It will be a great photo op when we reach the top!" he called over his shoulder. "Hope everyone brought their cameras!"

Chapter Six

"Say cheese, now!" Ted pressed a button on his digital camera, and a lightbulb flashed. He was going around taking pictures of each couple as they sipped their evening drinks on the outdoor patio on the second floor of their rustic hotel.

Eve was taking it easy tonight and drinking only sparkling water. Her head still spun from her horse ride up that mountain. If there'd been a view, she couldn't recall it. When they'd reached the top of that precipice, she'd nearly blacked out from fright. She must have participated somehow, because she had proof right here on her cell. Ted had offered to snap a shot, and there she sat, looking all natural and free like a regular horsewoman.

"Born to the saddle, you were," Scott teased. He was standing beside her and caught her stealing a glimpse at her phone. He was in the photo with her, sitting proudly on his horse. Scott really was a handsome man, broad across the shoulders and built rock solid. He had good manners and a fine sense of humor too. How she hated breaking the news to him.

Eve clicked off her phone and wedged it down in her purse. "I've never been so petrified," she confided. "I'm surprised I made it back here. Alive, I mean."

Scott chuckled and swigged from his beer just as Ted approached. "Your turn!" he said, angling his camera toward them.

"Oh no, I'm—" Eve fingered her hair, which was still in knots. It had been tangled in masses during her wild pony ride, fine clumps of curls wending their way around each other. The only solution was a shampoo and deep conditioning. In the short fifteen-minute breather she'd been allowed in her room, there hadn't been time.

She'd jumped in the shower to scrub off her horse scent and slipped into a sundress and sandals. On her way out the door, she'd grabbed a sweater too. Once night fell, it was bound to get cooler. She'd thought of putting up her hair, but for that reason left it down. She'd shaken it out a little and stared in the mirror. It actually looked okay, except for that tiny sprig of pine. She'd picked that out, hoping there were no more around back. Not that anyone would likely notice.

Scott leaned toward her and whispered, "You look gorgeous."

Eve caught Ted's gaze on her, which seem to hold agreement, and her cheeks warmed. That was probably part of his job. Making the brides feel lovely. Having them feel dowdy clearly wouldn't do. Not when he was hoping they would say *I do* to their matches at the end of their time here.

"Nothing like fresh air to bring out someone's natural beauty," Ted said. Then he motioned them a little closer. They stood by the outdoor fire pit, which Eve imagined could do a hearty service in winter. She'd heard Wyoming got frigid, even, at times, several degrees below zero. Thankfully, they were here in summer, and the breezes were balmy.

Scott caught her off guard by wrapping his arm around her. He hugged her to him as Ted's camera snapped one…two…three times.

"These are good ones," Ted proclaimed, displaying the camera before them as evidence. "I'll send you both copies."

"Great," Scott said before Eve added her thanks. When Ted went on to Gayle and Stephen, Scott said, "So tell me, Eve. What made you sign up for Wild West Brides?"

"I uh...actually." She gathered her nerve and, for a moment, wished she was drinking Chablis instead of water. "I was going to talk with you about that."

But instead of meeting her eyes, his gaze was fixed behind her. "How about that."

Eve turned to see people wearing some sort of winged contraptions jumping off the ridge of a nearby mountain. They took to the air and soared like birds, colorful gliders outstretched in the evening wind as the sun dipped behind them.

"It's called paragliding," Scott informed her. "We're going to do it too."

"W- w-w-wwweeee?"

"Day five."

Scott studied her. "Didn't you read your brochure?"

"Of course I read it! It's just that I... I thought the outings were optional."

"You're not afraid of heights?"

"Just a little." She eyed the men in the sky. "Heights like that, definitely."

"That's okay," he said with assurance. "There's plenty more to do. Like rafting on the Snake River."

Eve's brain couldn't get past the word *snake*. "There aren't really snakes in there?"

Scott laughed like he'd never considered it. "Now, Eve," he said. "Don't tell me you're backing out of rafting too?"

"No, it's just that..." Eve fidgeted with a lock of hair, and the back of her neck flashed hot. "I'm not such a great swimmer."

Scott smiled warmly. "I'm certified in first aid."

Now Eve's neck was on fire. Maybe if she told Scott the truth, he wouldn't be so pushy. Pushy about pushing her into things. Poor Scott, she almost felt sorry for him. One way or another, he almost seemed to like her, though Eve couldn't fathom why. Just then, Scott's cell rang, and he checked the number.

"Sorry," he told her. "I'm going to have to take this." Then he stepped into the building, leaving Eve alone. She glanced around, seeing the other couples had taken seats together and were chatting comfortably over drinks. Even Danni seemed to be opening up, her countenance starting to ease. Ted must have noted Eve had been temporarily abandoned and sauntered over to check in.

"Having fun so far?" His eyes were darker than brown. Nearly black. And they had a way of sparkling with mischief from time to time, like they were right now.

"Oh yes. It's been great! I mean, apart from the...rocky start." She dropped her chin. "I'm really sorry about the horse thing earlier."

"No problem. It happens."

"Really?"

"Yeah," he said. "Actually, it happens a lot." For a second, he appeared serious. Then his lips twitched in a grin.

"Ted Walker!" she scolded, teasing. "You know it doesn't."

"Okay, all right. I will admit that was a very unique spin on riding sidesaddle."

Eve couldn't pinpoint what seemed different about him, but something did. That struck her as a very glib comment for a cowboy. But maybe she was being unfair and patronizing. "You have quite a way with words, Mr. Walker."

"And you would know. You're a brochure writer?"

Eve thought quickly to what she'd put on her Wild West Brides application form. "For the travel industry. That's right."

"Do you work for a certain agency, or—"

"Oh look!" she said, glancing over her shoulder. "Here comes Scott!" But as he approached, she noted his expression was glum.

"Is everything all right?" Eve asked with concern.

His normally sunny face was dark and brooding. "It's Cathy, my little girl."

Ted addressed Scott. "I hope everything's okay."

"She's broken her arm, I'm afraid," Scott told them. "Fell off her bike this morning."

Eve's heart ached for the little girl having an accident when her father was away. "Oh no!"

"Yeah," Scott said, "I feel really bad about it. I'm all that Cathy's got. Her mom, she… Well, she isn't in the picture. Cathy was staying with her best friend's family so I could come here. It was the friend's mom who called."

Ted gave a worried frown. "I'm sorry, Scott. Really sorry to hear that."

Scott glanced at Eve, then sent Ted a telling look. "Do you mind if I have word with Eve?"

"No, of course not." Ted backed away. "Please let me know if there's anything I can do."

Eve studied him with understanding. He didn't have to say it; it was written in his eyes. "You need to go to her, don't you?"

"If it were anything less serious…" But his expression showed there was nothing more serious in the world. His baby girl was hurting, and he had to be there. Eve couldn't help but admire him for it.

"You don't have to explain it to me, Scott. I totally understand. Really, I do. Besides…" She felt her face warm with the admission. "I don't really believe it could have worked out for us anyway."

He eyed her curiously. "No?"

"You're from Montana, I'm from New York—"

"Then why'd you sign up for Wild West Brides?"

She drew a deep breath, searching for answers, but all the ones she'd prepared earlier evaded her. Scott's gaze was on her, waiting...wondering...

"It's not you, it's me!" she finally spouted.

Scott cocked his sturdy chin and folded his arms across his chest. "Eve," he said sternly. "Is something going on?"

She felt like a kid who'd been caught red-handed sneaking extra sweets. Darn. She wished she hadn't thought that. Made a craving for Milky Milanos come on strong. Thank goodness she'd stashed a bag in her suitcase.

Scott's raised his eyebrows. "Eve?"

"I'm not exactly sure what you mean."

He looked her up and down, then sharply angled his head like a cat sniffing out a rat. "You never intended to be a part of the program really, did you?"

"Shhh!" She stepped toward him and lowered her voice. "Scott, listen..." Suddenly, she realized she nearly stood on his toes. The distance between them had to be less than a foot. He stared down at her with light brown eyes. It occurred to Eve they were the color of acorns. A medium, sunny brown. Her gaze flitted to Ted, who was chatting amiably with the others. "You can't say a thing," she said, her eyes back on Scott's. "Especially not to my sister."

"Your sister?"

The back of Eve's neck flashed hot. "She's the one who put me up to it."

"What are you doing with your hair?"

Eve suddenly realized she'd subconsciously twisted it up. A pen poked out of Scott's pocket, and she desperately had to have it. "Do you mind?"

She indicated the pen, and he handed it over, taking care not to dislodged the paper he'd wedged in his pocket beside it. Eve figured he'd been taking notes during his phone call.

She secured her French twist with the pen, and a cooling breeze hit her nape. "Ah, better."

Scott cocked his head. "Your sister? You were saying...?"

She pursed her lips, then plunged in headlong. "Scott, listen to me. You're an incredible man. A totally stand-up guy, from everything I've seen. I have no clue why you came here, because—from my estimation—you could very easily have any woman you wanted."

"Why, thanks. I think."

"My point is, that girl can't possibly be me."

"I'm starting to see that, yes."

"I mean, you need someone to truly appreciate you. Someone who's ready."

"Somehow this feels like a really big kiss-off."

"Didn't you just say you were leaving?"

"I did, but..." He hesitated a moment. "It occurred to me that we were never even given a chance. That maybe— given Wild West Brides' algorithms—we were paired together for a reason."

Algorithms? Eve wasn't sure how Ted had gleaned so much information from her simple sign-up form. It wasn't as if she'd given her favorite flavor of ice cream or anything. "I hardly think we provided enough information to tell."

He gaped at her in disbelief, and Eve's cheeks caught fire. And she should be embarrassed, shouldn't she?

Duping a very nice man like Scott into believing she'd come here in search of a mate. Not only was he a totally nice guy, he was also apparently a caring single dad. Eve's stomach felt sour, and she hated herself in that moment. Hated everything about what she was doing and this stupid assignment. Maybe she should give it up now.

"Look, Scott, the truth is I never really intended to be here," she told him sheepishly. "Not as a Wild West Bride."

After a beat, he said. "Is this a usual thing for you? Pretending to be something you're not? Toying with other people's emotions?"

"No, I…" But her words trailed off. Try as she might, she couldn't think up a logical-sounding explanation. Anything she might say would only make her look like an even more callous player to him.

Scott glanced in Ted's direction. "When were you planning on filling him in? *Ever?*"

"What? No. I mean, yes. I will. Absolutely. Tell him the truth. All of it."

"I don't know why you even took this trip, Eve. But when you did, you signed on the dotted line. All right, it might have been an electronic signature…" Electronic signature? What on earth was he talking about? "It was right there on the Wild West Brides agreement."

"Agreement?" She hadn't a clue what he was talking about. All she'd signed was that enormously detailed liability waiver, plus the basic information form Glenn had submitted with her payment. The one with the confidentiality clause, explaining only first names would be used.

"Don't pretend you didn't read it."

"No, I… Well, of course I did! I…think."

He stopped her with a look, and suddenly his eyes didn't appear so warm. "Wow. You're good." Then he turned away, and Eve realized he was leaving. She felt sick to her stomach, as if she was the most horrible person on earth. And, in truth, maybe she was. She called weakly after him, "Scott...?"

He turned on his heels to glance at her for just a second. "You can keep the pen," he said without smiling. Then he strode toward Ted to inform him about the situation with his daughter and arrange his departure.

Chapter Seven

Eve bolted from the patio and tore for her room, tears burning down her cheeks. What a stupid idea this had been! *Stupid, stupid, stupid!* She couldn't believe she'd ever let Ross and Glenn con her into it. And what was that whole business about the agreement Scott alluded to? Eve sped past a gaggle of guests in the upstairs sitting room gathered around a colorful display of paintings and sipping chilled wine. An attractive blonde woman seemed to be holding court. A very handsome light-haired man and a small girl with a head of golden curls flanked her. Eve took them to be the artist with her family.

She and Scott had examined the paintings on their way out to the patio. Beautiful desert landscapes dotted with cacti, looming mesas, and towering buttes. Now they all melted in a swirl of tears. Thankfully, the group was too intent on the show and the artist to pay much mind to a weepy redhead with locks bouncing down her back as she fled.

Gratefully reaching her room, she let herself inside and shut the door behind her with a whimper. Why oh why had she done this? *To get promoted to Winnie's job, that's why*, she told herself sternly. She had to pull herself together and get a grip. Things weren't really as bad as they seemed. Scott was leaving anyway, and she still had time to get the low-down on Wild West Brides.

Eve drew a breath, then let it out—slowly. Her gaze caught on the new bag of Milky Milanos in her open suitcase. Her stomach rumbled. Thank goodness she'd thought ahead. That trail ride and all its excitement had left her incredibly hungry, and she'd barely touched the nice hors d'oeuvres Ted had set up outside. Eve crossed the room and reached for the cookie bag just as her cell rang.

"Glenn?"

"How's it going out there? Getting the scoop on Wild West Brides?" He sounded perky, probably from his lunchtime dose of caffeine. Glenn always did the double-shot latte.

Eve sank down on the bed and set the cookie bag on her knees. She popped the seal open. A delicious aroma wafted upward, and she drew in the smell, fairly well addicted. "I've been here less than a day."

"Right. One day out of seven. That means you've made headway, yeah?"

"That means I nearly flew off a horse!"

"What?"

"Thanks, Glenn. Thanks a lot." She dug her hand in the bag. "I very nearly died today on account of you."

He paused on the other end of the line before asking, "Is that crunching I hear?"

Eve studied the cookie in her hand, then glanced down at the bag, wondering where the Minicam was attached.

"Don't tell me you're eating Milky Milanos already?"

She chewed fast and swallowed. "Of course not. Just munching on some cheese and crackers from the hotel happy hour."

Eve pulled a tissue from the box beside the bed to wipe away her tears. There was something so soothing about chocolate. She felt better already.

"Well, good. That's good. Ross asked me to check in, and I said I would. I'll tell him things are moving along, then."

Eve blinked and set the cookie bag aside. "Uh..."

"They *are* moving, aren't they?"

"Yes! I'm getting a really great view from the inside. I'll be typing up some notes this evening."

"And sending them along, I hope?"

"Now, don't get anxious. And you can tell Ross to hold his horses too. I'll have the story when I have the story, but I'm not sharing until it's ready."

"Fine. He'll probably live with that."

Before they hung up, she asked, "Was there some sort of agreement about coming here? A contract or something?"

"Contract?"

"Another participant mentioned me having signed on the dotted line, but I don't recall—"

His laugh was affected. "Oh *that*! No problem. I took care of it for you when I was making your arrangements."

Eve gaped in disbelief. "You forged my signature?"

"Forged is such an ugly word."

"Glenn!"

"I was helping, Eve. There wasn't time."

"Time for what?"

"For you to read the fine print. Plus, there were all those nonsensical questions to answer."

"What questions?"

"Oh, you know… What's your favorite kind of ice cream, that kind of thing. Rum raisin, right?"

"Rum raisin? No! Where on earth did you get that?"

She could almost see him shrug through the phone.

"Same place I got most of the answers, from my cousin Debbie."

"Debbie-the-dancer Debbie?"

"No, the dancer's name is Sandy. Debbie works at—"

"I don't really care! I just can't believe you gave her information as mine. What were you thinking?"

He huffed a breath. "Only that I had less than a day to make your arrangements, and you couldn't book without completing that ridiculous questionnaire for their algorithms."

"Algorithms. I see."

"I didn't give all her answers. Just most of them. She's the only woman I know well enough to—"

Eve's heart sank. Maybe she didn't want to know the rest. "What about the agreement?" she asked softly. "What exactly did you sign me up for?"

"To tell you the truth, I really can't—"

She pulled back the phone and stared at it, then grated into the receiver, *"Glenn..."*

"Okay. All right already. It was just something silly. Some kind of pledge attesting to the fact that you are single and available—which I happen to know you are—and that you're open to accepting proposals of marriage. Which you certainly should be at your advanced age."

She took exception to Glenn painting her as an old maid. Just because he was in his midtwenties, that didn't make her ancient by comparison.

"I'm barely thirty-one!"

"And, something about no communicable diseases— but I didn't feel it my business to ask, because truthfully, since you're not staying, it doesn't matter anyway. *And,* that you're promising Wild West Brides you won't make any rash decisions."

"Is that it?"

"Well, there's that little thing about your commitment to your assigned match, even if unforeseen circumstances should drive you apart. You're agreeing to see that person for the full five dates, in—or outside of—Wyoming. Or at least remain open to that possibility.

"Honestly," he said in a confidential tone, "I think that Ted guy is very sure of his program."

A heavy feeling settled in Eve's belly. That was why Scott was so put out. He couldn't help that he had to leave, but he'd still hoped they'd make up the rest of the week somehow. He'd agreed to that in advance. Apparently, he'd thought she had as well.

Well, she'd put the kibosh on that, hadn't she? And with very good reason, Eve reminded herself. She wasn't here to become legitimately involved. She was here to do research. Besides, Scott was a very nice man and a caring single dad. He certainly deserved better than her. And she clearly wasn't prepared to move to Montana!

Still, she felt guilty about hurting his feelings and not being honest with him from the start. Though it had been pretty hard to think about anything else when she'd been clinging for dear life to the saddle horn of a horse.

She hung up with Glenn, just as someone knocked on her door.

Ted stood outside of Eve's room, worrying over what had gone wrong. Naturally, she was upset about Scott leaving. The two had seemed suitably matched and had gotten off to a reasonable start. He'd hated that she'd been so upset when she'd fled from the patio. As the other couples hadn't noticed her departure, he'd tried not to make a point of it. Instead, he'd casually excused himself after setting up everyone's arrangements for tomorrow. A few seconds passed, and he wondered if she was going to answer. It occurred to him that maybe she wasn't even here. Perhaps, rather than going back to her room, she'd headed downstairs to the bar or else out on the town somewhere.

He was turning to go when her door popped open. She looked a mess. Her red curls were in disarray, and tiny crumbles of something lined the top of her bodice. Plus, it was clear she'd been crying. Evidently, a lot. It was the damndest thing that she could still look beautiful. Yet somehow she did. Stunning when those big brown eyes peered up at him, even though they were tinged with sadness.

After her crazy antics on that horse, Ted had scarcely been able to take his eyes off her on the trail. Though he'd known it was wrong, and that Eve was Scott's appointed match, he hadn't been able to help stealing peeks at her over his shoulder. He told himself it was because she was a klutz and he feared she'd get thrown from her horse. But his soul knew something different. There'd been something in her quirky, whimsical ways that had called to him. But he'd cautioned himself not to answer. Ted had no business being interested in one of his brides. And look how devastated she was! Scott's leaving had obviously hit her very hard.

"I just wanted to check on you," he said. "I'm sorry, Eve. So sorry about Scott."

She sniffed a little and wiped the crumbs from her dress. "It was one of those things that couldn't be helped."

"Are you okay?"

She bit her lower lip. After a beat, she said, "Yeah. Fine."

He folded his arms across his chest. "You don't look fine."

The color in her cheeks deepened.

"I didn't mean you don't look good," he corrected. "Great. Awesome!" Suddenly, he remembered he was a cowboy. "Just as right as a filly after the rain."

Eve pointedly arched an eyebrow. "I'd appreciate it very much if you didn't bring up horses."

"You actually did okay. I was impressed with the way you handled the rest of the ride."

"Meaning you were glad I didn't fall off."

His lips parted in a grin. "That too."

"Ted, about Scott—"

"No problem," he rushed in. "You'll still get the full five dates. It's in the—"

She met his eyes. "You don't understand. I don't want them."

Ted paused to consider this. Brian's computer program had never failed to make a match. Most had been perfect. "You weren't...?" He lowered his voice as a couple passed behind him in the hall. "You're not attracted to Scott?"

"He's a really great guy."

"Just not the guy for you?"

Ted quickly puzzled this through. *Impossible!* Something had gone wrong, undeniably wrong, in the match they'd made between Scott and Eve. But what? Ted spoke, still at a loss. "Brian's computer program is nearly foolproof."

"Nearly isn't one hundred percent. Look, I already talked to Scott and told him. He knows there's no future between us."

Ted's head spun. He and Brian had become so cocky about their program, it was as if they held a flat assumption it would work. Yet, on an intellectual level, both realized that expectation was unrealistic. Hadn't they discussed a situation like Eve's potentially occurring some day?

"Well, I'm sorry. Really sorry to hear that." He was too, especially since she hadn't given Scott very much time. Less than a full day hardly seemed long enough to reach a decision. "Are you sure you wouldn't want to try again? Give Scott another chance after—"

"I really appreciate what you're doing, but I think it's better if I just—"

"You want a refund, don't you."

"What?"

"I can return your money, if that's what you want."

"That's not what I want."

He blinked with comprehension. Was Eve actually intending to stay? But why? It occurred to Ted that maybe Eve's situation with Scott might have caught her off guard too. Eve might have believed herself ready to meet someone and make a commitment, but when she'd arrived here, she'd gotten cold feet. That wouldn't mean she thought Scott was a bad guy, but it could make her hesitant about pursuing a relationship. Perhaps it took coming to Jackson Hole for Eve to realize she wasn't truly prepared to think hearts and wedding bells. Still, he had to make sure it was that and not something else.

"You don't have a partner, you know," he said gently. "And it's really too late for me to bring in someone else."

"That's okay. I don't mind doing the adventures on my own."

This was completely unprecedented. He and Brian had never had a bride stick around without the groom before. Then again, Eve had paid her money just like the rest of the group. If she wanted to see the week through, that was her prerogative, wasn't it? Frankly, Ted admired her gumption. What's more, he figured his first guess had been right. Eve Parker was no more interested in becoming involved with anyone right now than he was.

"You won't be completely on your own. You'll have the rest of us there."

Eve shifted on her feet. "I appreciate you understanding."

Actually, he was still trying to wrap his head around it. But he knew in some ways it was none of his business. Even if he *was* the director of Wild West Brides, Ted wasn't always privy to the inner workings of the human heart.

He tipped his hat toward her.

"I guess I'll see you tomorrow, then."

"Wild West Safari," she said, apparently remembering.

"We leave from the lobby at four."

Her voice rose. "*A.M.?*"

"Best time to catch those elk and moose."

She looked doubtful but forced a smile. "Right."

"Try to get some shut-eye," he said with a wink.

Chapter Eight

Eve awoke to a loud pounding. *Is that thunder?* She rolled over with a groan. *Yeow!* Every inch of her body ached. Her hips were sore, her shoulders hurt, and her inner thighs throbbed. *Bang, bang, bang!* There it was again. She peered through the darkness at the digital clock on the nightstand. Four a.m. *Huh?* Then she remembered.

"Eve?" a husky voice called. "Are you in there?"

Eve sat bolt upright in bed, her muscles painfully clenching. Oh no! *Ted.* She was supposed to be downstairs meeting everybody in the lobby. *Knock, knock, knock!*

Eve slid her feet from the covers and set them on the floor. *Ow, ow, ouch! Ow, Mama!* Bolts of pain shot up her legs as she stood, causing her to double forward. "Coming!" She tentatively put one foot in front of the other, walking with wobbly steps, her knees angled out sideways. No wonder cowboys were bowlegged! Aspirin, she had to find aspirin. Acetaminophen. Something! She could barely breathe from the pain. It was that trail ride, she realized. Not to mention her unforgettable introduction to the horse.

She set her hand on the doorknob and yanked it open. Ted studied her with surprise. "Rise and…shine?"

Eve suddenly realized she looked a mess. There she stood in her ratty pajama pants and T-shirt, hair tangled in an unruly mass. She tried to run her fingers through it, but they caught—and stuck. Eve stared at Ted in horror, her right hand plastered to her head. Wait! Was there something in there? Something wedged deep in her curls?

Ted leaned toward her, and Eve froze. What was he doing standing so close? And why did he smell so good at four in the morning? All manly and sensual, like he'd bathed in musk oil or some kind of scented soap? Eve questioned whether she was still dreaming, because she'd envisioned him all night long. She wondered if he'd thought of her also, but then realized that was ludicrous. Yet, maybe it wasn't. Here he was, outside her room, way before sunrise, looking like sin and smelling delectable. Tastier than a big, sticky cinnamon bun. Eve licked her lips, thinking she'd like a taste of *him* with her coffee.

He must have been thinking the same thing about her, because he was drawing nearer, his mouth homing in on hers. Their gazes locked, and Eve's temperature spiked. His eyes were dark and sultry, like he hungered for her too. This was it, their moment of truth. He obviously didn't give a damn about that safari, or about Wild West Brides. All he wanted was one hot reporter from Brooklyn... *Wait! Ted doesn't know that.*

Ted slowly raised a hand, and Eve's heart pounded. Was he going to cup her chin? Pull her smack up against him? She tried not to imagine getting swept into his arms, but her mind went there anyway. Went there and stayed there, with her unbuttoning his shirt.

Something pinged at her scalp. "Ouch!"

"Looking for this?" Ted asked, producing the pen he'd plucked from her hair.

Eve's face flushed. "Um, yeah. Thanks."

For a moment, Ted appeared lost, like he'd had something on the tip of his tongue but then had forgotten what he was going to say. He absentmindedly lowered the pen in his hand while talking. "Why aren't you downstairs? Aren't you coming with us?"

"You're not wearing your cowboy hat?" she asked, noting it suddenly.

"Don't need it before daylight," he explained. "It's in the SUV. Although I do have my camera." He started to pull it from his pocket as proof, and a horrible thought flashed through Eve's brain. He could take a photo of her now and document her unglamorous moment. Her unglamorous—and delusional—moment! *What was I thinking?*

She laid her hand on his and shoved the camera back down in his shirt. "I believe you!" she said before wincing in pain.

He angled his head with concern. "Are you okay?"

Eve rubbed her aching bum. "Just a little saddle sore from yesterday."

"Well, it's no wonder." He stopped himself. "What I mean is…you had quite a ride. Especially at the beginning."

"Yes." She eyed him apologetically. "Ted, I'm really sorry. I should have called. But I don't think I can possibly…" She shifted on her feet and sucked in a breath. "Hoo, boy."

Ted lifted his brow. "Pretty bad, huh?"

She nodded, not daring to move again.

"You probably need a soak," he told her. "Hot bath and maybe some analgesics. Do you have any?"

"In my suitcase."

"Take two, and I'll call you later."

"Call me?" she asked weakly.

"To see how you're doing."

"Oh right."

"I'm serious about that hot bath."

Eve had the crazy notion she wouldn't mind having him in it with her. Suddsing up her shoulders and massaging her aching back. Eve mentally slapped herself. She must have missed something he'd said.

"Um, right. I'll be sure to take two with a glass of water as soon as I shut the door."

His face registered surprise. "You're going to eat bath salts?"

"What? No! Ha-ha…" She took a step backward and winced. "Tiny joke there."

"Good one. Very funny."

He grinned, and Eve's tailbone tingled.

"Well, take care of yourself then."

"Thanks, I will."

"Just take it easy for now."

"Okay."

"We'll hook up later."

Eve's face burned.

Ted nearly tripped, walking backward. "I meant connect. Talk. By telephone. Cell." He turned and headed for the stairs. "Have a good bath!"

Ted took the steps two at a time, chiding himself. *Have a good bath? Seriously? You said that?* He didn't know what it was about Eve that left him all tongue-tied this morning. Maybe it was the cute way she looked in her pajamas with her hair all a mess. Or maybe it was the silly way that pen had been poking out of her hair like some sort of alien antenna. She'd appeared sleepy and befuddled and more than a little worn thin from her previous day's adventures. He couldn't blame her for wanting to take today off to recover. But secretly, he was disappointed she wouldn't be joining them for the safari. While the initial news about her and Scott not working out had been a shock, the more Ted had thought about it, the better he'd felt about that outcome. It was clearly best to have no match than to be paired with the wrong person. Now that he'd reflected on it, he could see Scott wasn't the man for

Eve at all. It was a good thing she'd seen that too and had called things off before it was too late.

He hated that the situation had proved awkward for the couple but believed they'd both get over it and move on. Scott certainly had a lot going for him. As did Eve. She was smart and pretty and sexy, despite that quirky little thing she did with her hair. He thought he'd imagined her putting it up with Scott's pen last night. But when he'd found it in her hair this morning, well... Ted chuckled, buoyed by the thought of seeing her later. He'd check in on her to see how she was doing. That was part of his role in overseeing Wild West Brides. He had to ensure all his guests were safe and comfortable.

Ted rounded the corner to the lobby, and Brian met his gaze with a knowing look. "Not coming, is she?"

"Eve's going to take it easy today," Ted told the waiting group.

As they headed toward the large SUV in the parking lot, Brian leaned toward Ted with a whisper. "What exactly is going on?"

"I don't know what you mean."

"I'm talking about you, man." Brian wagged a finger. "You're acting strange."

"Am I?"

"Darn right you are." He curiously eyed his friend in the darkness, his gaze glancing at Ted's hand. "And where did you get that pen?"

Ted slipped it in his pocket beside his digital camera. "I thought I might need it," he lied. "You know, in case I have to take notes."

"Sure you will." Brian glanced toward the hotel and the darkened windows upstairs. "But something tells me what you want to study is up there."

"Don't be ridiculous," Ted snapped under his breath. "I haven't hit on a Wild West Bride yet, and I don't intend to start now." And he wouldn't, Ted told himself sternly. From here on out, things between him and Eve would remain strictly professional. Not that they'd been anything *but* until now.

"You taking her to dinner tonight?" Brian asked after they'd loaded the others in the SUV and shut their doors.

"Actually, I hadn't thought about it."

"Well, you better start thinking soon. Scott left, remember? As far as I can tell, Eve's dinner dance card is empty."

Ted swallowed hard, realizing it was. Brian was absolutely right. With Scott gone, Ted would need to fill in. Not as a match for Eve. No, no. Nothing like that. But as a dinner date? Adventure partner? Sure, that made sense. It was the best way to ensure Eve enjoyed the rest of her time here and didn't find Wyoming a total waste. Ted could do that and keep things on the up-and-up. He couldn't count on Brian to take up the slack. Brian's girlfriend, Mary, would never let him hear the end of it.

Ted patted the pen in his pocket, regretting the fact that he'd walked away with it. It only made him think of Eve and how adorable she'd looked standing in that doorway. No! He wouldn't go there. Couldn't. And he wasn't going to. Ted settled behind the wheel, and Brian slid into the passenger seat. "Ready to get this show on the road?" he asked the others in back.

"Yes, sir! Yehaw!" they answered excitedly en mass.

Ted caught a glimpse of Gayle snuggled up beside Stephen, and Danni sitting happily near Chet behind them. Well, at least this week was going great for two of the couples. *And, two out of three ain't bad...* Ted thought, humming the tune to a song.

Chapter Nine

Eve took two painkillers and hit the hay. That's the way Ted would have phrased it. Or so she thought. He wasn't quite as cowboy-like as she'd expected him to be. Then again, Eve wasn't sure what she'd been expecting. Some masked man with a Native American sidekick?

She gingerly rolled onto her side, every muscle aching. Perhaps she should have had that bath before trying to go back to sleep. Yet, she was too beat at the moment to do anything other than lie there and console her brittle body. *Ow!* Even moving under the covers smarted. She gathered the sheet a little more tightly around herself, and the room faded into a haze. In the distance, she heard hoof beats. The steady thundering of a horse galloping away. Or maybe that was rain outside, beating against her windowpane. Thunder rumbled loudly as Eve drifted off. *Yeah, probably thunder.*

Ted glanced over his shoulder and shot her a wink. "Hasn't got a thing on the thunder in my heart or the fire in my veins."

"Oh!" Eve held on tighter as they climbed high up the ridge to a precipice that looked not unlike the one Ted had taken them to yesterday morning. "Where are we going?" she asked, nearly breathless.

He reached down and stroked her hands as they circled his waist. "Someplace beautiful, darling."

Then they were there! Up on the summit, overlooking the valley below. Across the way, the Grand Teton Mountains appeared like the backdrop from a movie. Small, dark figures dotted the field below them.

"Wild buffalo," Ted explained as Eve watched with amazement.

"Real ones?"

"As real as they come." He carefully untwined her arms, then hopped off the horse, helping her down next. "I'll cook you a buffalo steak, if you'd like one."

She gazed up in his eyes, which smoldered in the waning light. It was sunset, she realized, and this time he was indeed wearing his hat. "Or maybe," he said, brushing his lips to hers. "You'd like a taste of cowboy?"

Tingles tore down Eve's spine, then rocketed right back up again. "Ted..." She sagged in his arms, but his steady embrace held her.

His breath raked her lips. "I'll give you anything you want. Anything...at all. No request is too big or too small."

She looked up in his eyes, unable to deny it. "You." Her words came out in a light whisper. "All I want is you, cowboy."

"Yeehaw," he said in a sexy growl, bringing his mouth to hers.

Eve's eyes popped open. What? Where? Her gaze panned to the bedside clock, and she saw it was past eleven. *Kaboom!* And it was thundering outside. Thundering and raining too. She could hear the rain streaming down in torrents, cascading against the building. She thought immediately of Ted and the group on the safari. What a dreadful morning for a ride. And what a crazy dream she'd had. Eve pushed herself up halfway in bed and shook out her curls. Maybe it was time she got in that bath and scrubbed such bubbleheaded notions from her brain. She and Ted on a horse! Hoo! *Wanna taste of cowboy?* Ha-ha.

Eve lowered her feet to the floor. *Argh.* She would have to watch it with Ted. But most importantly, she had to watch herself so as to not get carried away. She had a job to do, and she intended to do it well. After she soaked for a bit, she'd borrow an umbrella from the hotel concierge and check out the town. Now that she knew a little more about Wild West Brides, she could start thinking about how she might angle her article. Perhaps she could find a nice quiet spot where she could sit with a cup of coffee for a while and jot down some ideas.

Ted and Brian hurriedly corralled the others back in the SUV. Rain was pounding, and they'd all gotten drenched. Now they had to navigate this backwoods mountain road in a downpour. But Ted wasn't worried. He and Brian had done it dozens of times. Since he'd driven up, Brian took the wheel heading back. If Eve had ever picked a good day to play hooky, this was it. He turned in his seat to address the others in the back. "Everyone okay?"

To his surprise, Danni laughed. "Oh yeah, that was a blast!"

"What?"

Chet brought his arm around her and chuckled when water pouring off her slicker doused his leg. "That was an adventure, all right."

"Can't say what was better," Stephen added. "Getting rained out of a safari or our horse ride on the trail."

"I think they were both great." Gayle beamed up at him. "Each in its own way."

"That's what Wild West Brides is all about," Ted said surely. "Adding a little adventure to your life!"

"Yeah," Brian said quietly but not quietly enough, "and a whole lot of L-O-V-E."

There was dead silence for a moment, then the girls giggled while the men erupted in nervous laughter.

Brian shot Ted a look. "What?"

"Nothing, Bri," Ted said, shaking his head. "Nothing at all."

The bath helped a lot. By the time Eve climbed from the steaming water, her skin was wrinkled, but her muscles were soothed enough that she could walk again. She dressed in jeans and a light summer top, then pulled back the curtains. To her delight, the rain had stopped. A warm mist rose off the road dividing her homey hotel from a large central park, where a few random patrons walked their dogs. The sun didn't precisely beam, but it was emerging. She spied its edge peeking out from beyond the rim of a faraway cloud. *Guess I won't be needing that umbrella.*

Eve's stomach rumbled, and she realized how hungry she was. She hadn't had a thing to eat since those meager appetizers last night on the outdoor patio. Her gaze snagged on an empty cookie bag in the trash. *And, oh yeah, those.* Still, it was high noon. Those calories had long since worn off. And Eve was famished. She tucked a small notepad and a pen in her purse, then grabbed her cell and slipped out the door.

Chapter Ten

Eve exited her hotel and headed toward town, the smell of damp grass in the park across the way awakening her senses. The sun had come out in full force now and shimmered down upon the narrow city streets that crisscrossed toward the heart of Jackson Hole. She passed coffee shops, clothing boutiques, and eateries with outdoor tables still glistening with raindrops. There were no skyscrapers here. Just low buildings with a story or two, nestled up against Snow King Mountain. Even from her limited view with a slew of businesses in the way, she could tell its ski slopes were formidable. In summertime, its highest peaks formed perfect launching pads for paragliders. That was where she and Scott had witnessed people setting sail from last night.

Eve felt a slight ping in her heart, worrying over Scott. She'd really hated to disappoint him, but she'd never intended to be a bride anyway. What's more, she didn't feel that certain chemistry she'd hoped to find with a man some day. She'd had that with Gustavo in Spain. Yet, in the end, pure physical attraction hadn't been enough. She'd thought they'd been getting to know and trust each other. That maybe Gustavo was developing more than fleeting feelings for her. Never mind that she wasn't 100 percent certain in her feelings for him.

Her friend Jessica had initially felt confused during her whirlwind romance with the matador. The fact that it began with an accidental marriage had only heightened her anxiety. Eve had been worried sick over the situation too. Was her best friend since eighth grade getting sucked into a situation where she was in way over her head? Eve had tried to rush to her aid, but Jess had bristled at that, indicating no help was needed. Jess's instincts had proven right. Now just look at her! With an idyllic life in Spain, an adoring—not to mention rich and incredibly sexy— husband, and a new toddler daughter that Eve had only met through Skype.

"Megan! Come out of the way!"

Eve looked down and saw she'd nearly trampled a little girl holding a big, dripping ice-cream cone. Her mother tugged the child aside with an apologetic look. The mom had chin-length blonde hair cut in a cute, angled bob and big dark eyes like her daughter's. "I'm so sorry. Sometimes she doesn't pay—" Eve recognized her at once from the hotel. A tall, handsome man stood beside her with a pleasant smile and a golden brown tan.

"Aren't you staying back at the Oasis?" Eve asked them.

The woman blinked, clearly trying to place her. "Why, yes. Yes, we are. And you are?"

Eve held out her hand. "Eve Parker. We haven't met, but I thought I saw you at the art opening."

"That was my Gwen, all right," the man said proudly, hugging her shoulder. He shook Eve's hand. "Dan Holbrook."

His wife spoke next. "Gwendolyn Marsh, professionally. But it's Gwen Holbrook in my personal life." She smiled down at her curly headed daughter, who looked to be five or six years old. "And this is Megan."

"Well, hello, Megan," Eve said sweetly. "How's that ice cream? Pretty yummy, I'll bet." It had to be. She'd apparently been enjoying it a lot. It was smeared all over her chin.

The child lowered her eyes and nodded shyly.

"She's a little quiet around strangers," Gwen told her. "But she can sing at the top of her lungs once she gets to know you."

"Sing?" Eve laughed lightly. "I'll bet she sounds like an angel."

"That she does," Dan added. He sent an appreciative glance toward his wife. "Just like her mom."

Gwen elbowed him. "Shush!" She turned her attention on Eve. "He's just ribbing me, you know. I couldn't carry a tune in a bucket."

Eve smiled at the happy family. What a pretty picture they made. "I caught a glimpse of your work last night," she told Gwen. "Now that I've met the artist in person, I'll have to go back and take a closer look."

Gwen flushed at the compliment. "Please do. I hope you'll like them. They're mostly desert landscapes."

"Of New Mexico," Dan filled in. "She paints at our ranch."

"How lovely," Eve said, meaning it. She couldn't imagine what that might be like, doing something as creative and wonderful as crafting original paintings, and having a warm, supportive family besides. She glanced down at Megan, who was shuffling her feet. "I didn't mean to keep you."

"No trouble," Dan said.

Gwen's smile was genuine and warm. "It was really great to meet you, Eve. Are you in town for long?"

"Just this week. How about you?"

"We're headed home in the morning."

"Well, enjoy the rest of your stay, then."

"Thanks, you too."

The family started moving past her on the sidewalk when a thought occurred. Eve had a friend who ran a small gallery in Chelsea. He was always looking for interesting pieces and enjoyed highlighting artwork from different locales. While she hadn't examined Gwen's work up close, maybe she should get Gwen's card just in case. What if her paintings were fantastic? Wouldn't that be a neat twist of fate? Eve might actually accomplish some good on this trip and leave someone feeling happy rather than upset and disappointed. "Wait!"

All three turned and glanced over their shoulders. "Your paintings... I mean, are you open to exhibits? Things like that?"

Gwen turned to fully face her. "Why, yes, of course," she said, appearing mildly perplexed.

"I was just thinking..." Eve ran her fingers through her hair. "What I'm saying is, I've got a friend with a gallery in New York. It's a small one, but still—"

Gwen's face broadened in a big, beaming smile, her blonde bob bouncing. "That would be awesome! Thanks so much, Eve."

"I'll give it a shot, though I can't make any promises."

"Of course not." Gwen dug in her bag and pulled a business card from a slim container. "But I sure appreciate the thought."

Eve's heart felt light. It was that good kind of feeling that came from helping someone. "I'll be sure to take a closer look at your paintings this evening. Maybe photograph a few before you go."

"That's fine, thank you. Although you don't have to worry about the paintings leaving with us. When we go, they're staying behind—for at least a few more weeks. Plus, I've got slides of them all uploaded to my website." She handed over her card, and Eve slid it into her purse.

"Super, thanks. Safe travels."

"You too."

"Don't forget the cowboys!" a little voice piped in.

Eve looked down at Megan, who met her gaze with big brown eyes.

"The cowboys are shooting! Over there!" She pointed with her ice cream toward the distant town square.

Dan gave a low chuckle. "It's something they put on for the tourists," he said quietly to Eve.

"I'll be sure to check it out," she told the child. "If there's anything I love, it's a cowboy!"

Eve said good-bye to the Holbrooks and strode toward the main square, her bag slung over her shoulder. She spied a commotion up ahead where a crowd had gathered in the street. Families lined the road and children sat on the split-rail fence circling the town square. Eve approached it, seeing that each entranceway to the central green was charmingly crafted of elk antlers. They interlinked and towered high, their bone-colored arches offsetting an azure sky. A clapboard sign hung overhead, proudly proclaiming *Jackson Hole*.

A shot rang out, and Eve stopped in her tracks. Men were shouting at each other.

"Hold it right there, partner!"

"Not on your life, you slimy snake!"

Bang! There it went again.

The crowd gasped and cheered as the saloon villain fell to his knees, clutching his side with an exaggerated frown. Actors were staging a showdown, and the watching tourists loved it. This was part of the Wild West appeal of Jackson Hole. A reminder of how the rogue town might have operated in the olden days. *When men were men, and women were glad.* Eve startled at that thought, wondering where it had come from.

Even as she pondered this, she saw him approaching. He walked with a purposeful air, powering forward in jeans and a dark T-shirt that did everything to outline the contours of his muscled chest. Ted tipped his Stetson and smiled at some children picnicking on the lawn with their family. "Howdy!"

Little faces beamed as their parents shared polite hellos. Eve wanted to move, needed to walk. But she stayed nailed in place, mesmerized. Ted wasn't just handsome; he was drop-dead gorgeous. And, he was walking right up to her! Dark eyes snagged on hers and sparkled. "Eve Parker," he said with a grin. "This *is* a surprise."

Eve caught her breath and tried to sound nonplussed. "A surprise that I'm up and walking, you mean?"

His gaze traveled over her body. Was she imagining it, or was there something sultry in his perusal? "How you holding up?"

"Doing better." She adjusted the bag on her shoulder with a laugh. "The extra rest really helped." She'd been about to mention the bath but then thought better of it. Best to keep any thoughts of her and Ted hitting the suds together at bay. Far, far away... Eve swallowed hard, remembering her nutty dream.

He angled his hat in her direction. "Gotta say, you picked the right day to skip a safari."

"Get caught in the rain?"

"More like *drenched*. But the others didn't seem to mind." His eyes locked on hers, and Eve's temperature spiked. She'd give anything to twist up her hair, but didn't dare move a muscle. Already her palms felt slick and were losing their grip on the strap of her bag.

"I'm glad everyone seems to be getting along. Sounds like it's turning out to be a good week for Wild West Brides. "

"Yup."

"I mean, in spite of..."

He studied her face, and Eve's pulse pounded. "In spite of what happened with me and Scott."

"It's funny you should mention that," he began.

"Oh?"

"Yeah. About the rest of the week—"

She was trying to listen, but Eve had something pressing on her mind. A confession. "Ted, I need to talk to you about something."

This was it. She was going to spill it. Eve could no longer pretend she'd come here to meet her perfect match. She'd come here to do a story, plain and simple. And she was going to tell him. The cards would just have to fall as they would.

They stepped aside as people bustled past them on the walk. The street theatrics had ended, and now the crowd was dispersing.

"Perfect!" he said with a grin. "You can tell me all about it at dinner."

"Dinner?"

"Tonight was supposed to be your first evening out with Scott. Seeing as how he's not here, I'd hate for you to have to go it alone."

"I really don't mind… What I mean is—"

"Eve," he said with a serious stare, "I feel I owe it to you. By all accounts, your first twenty-four hours with Wild West Brides were a disaster."

"I wouldn't call them a disaster, so much."

"You nearly fell off your horse, your date ditched you—"

"He didn't exactly ditch. I mean, it wasn't his—"

"*And* you woke up unable to move."

"Well, when you put it that way…"

A slow grin crept across his handsome face. "Let me make it up to you. Just a little. A good steak and a bottle of wine. You can tell me whatever it is you wanted to talk about then. He surveyed her eyes for clues. "That is, unless it's pressing."

Eve had to admit the idea of sharing a meal with Ted did sound appealing. She hadn't had a date since goodness knew when. Her last few outings had been fix-ups and utterly disastrous ones at that. Not that dining with Ted would be a date or anything. She did have to eat, Eve told herself reasonably. And she'd gone clear through that bag of Milky Milanos.

"Okay."

"Okay?" His brow creased slightly. "Was that a yes?"

Eve's heart thumped. Why did she feel so petrified? Like a teenager getting asked out for the very first time? She nodded and tried to mutter something intelligible but only came out with, "Um-hum."

"That's dandy!" He held her gaze. "I'll meet you in your hotel lobby at eight."

Eve suddenly got cold feet, like she couldn't go through with this. She needed to tell Ted and tell him now. Not have him take her out to dinner as if she were some poor, forlorn woman who'd missed her last chance at love. *Or maybe I am some poor, forlorn woman who's missed her last chance at love.* Eve bit her lower lip to keep it from trembling. Her life was a mess. Maybe she really should have been a Wild West Bride. Was it so wrong to want that kind of happiness? The happiness the sunny faces of all those couples proclaimed to have found in Ted's neat array of glossy brochures?

"If eight's too late," he said, misreading her silence, "I can come by sooner."

But Eve couldn't tell him yet. Not now, not here, not in the middle of the Jackson Hole town square. She needed time to think this through and explain it in a way that didn't make her look so terrible. For, whether she understood it or not, Eve cared what Ted thought about her. "No, that's great." She forced a pleasant grin and gripped her bag. "Eight will be fine."

Ted walked away from Eve, a light spring in his step. He didn't know what he was so darn happy about. Taking Eve to dinner was merely his professional obligation. One he might not even had thought of if Brian hadn't suggested it. Ted angled his hat to shield his eyes from the streaming sun, knowing that was bunk. *I would have thought of it, all right. Thought of it and been more than a little envious of Scott if he'd been the one taking Eve out.*

Ted was almost ashamed to admit that he was happy one of his Wild West setups had fallen through. But in his heart, he couldn't help but believe things had worked out that way for a reason. He wondered what Eve wanted to talk about, but figured she might want to apologize. Though Ted understood it wasn't really her fault. You couldn't always help who you were attracted to. Sometimes it just wasn't there. At others, it could hit you like a ton of bricks.

Ted recalled Eve's crazy antics on her horse and suppressed a chuckle. While he'd worried for her safety at the time, in retrospect the occasion presented a very memorable moment. In fact, he'd likely recall it for the rest of his life. Ted's Adam's apple rose and fell as he realized what he'd been thinking. And what he'd been thinking of was knowing Eve forever. For long enough into the future that both of them could some day look back to the start of this week and laugh.

But that was an absurd thought to have. Eve was here for one week and one week only. And if she hadn't found her perfect mate in Scott, that was a shame, but there was nothing Ted could do about it. Other than keep her company and help ease the sting of disappointment. Even if he couldn't understand why the match between Eve and Scott had failed, Ted was smart enough to sense the situation had been hard on both of them. Nobody joined up at Wild West Brides without secretly wishing for something. That a few outdoor adventures and some algorithms could fix a lonely heart—and, maybe even on the outside—mend a broken one.

Chapter Eleven

When Ted met Eve in her hotel lobby a little after eight, she looked incredible. She wore a pretty, curve-hugging sundress, and her hair was up, exposing an alabaster neck. She clutched a purse in her hand along with a light sweater, a good thought since temperatures around here were known to dip at night. "Hope you're in the mood for buffalo," he said with a grin.

Eve lifted her eyebrows. "Buffalo?"

"Steak," he explained. "Mesquite grilled. It's the best thing on the menu."

"Aren't they an endangered species or something?"

"Not around here." He led her toward the door and held it open. "That's right," he recalled. "I forgot you weren't with us on this morning's adventure."

"I didn't realize the Wild West safari included buffalo."

"Technically, they're really bison. Buffalo live in other parts of the world. But that whole Buffalo Bill thing? It really plays well for the tourists." They stepped onto the sidewalk, and he motioned in the direction they were headed.

Eve's lips turned down in a frown. "I'm kind of sorry I missed it. Are they really as huge as they appear in books?"

"I'll let you judge for yourself."

She stared at him in surprise.

"Tomorrow morning, on our way up to Jenny Lake. We'll drive right by the sagebrush meadows where lots of them graze."

Her face brightened momentarily, then she rubbed a sore hip. "Jenny Lake. That's the day hike, isn't it?"

"And a beautiful one at that. Tomorrow's going to be clear as a bell. Spectacular day for seeing the falls." He tried to disguise the worry in his eyes. "You are coming with us? I hope."

"If it involves seeing buffalo…ah, bison." She smiled pleasantly. "I wouldn't miss it."

"The lake's pretty special too."

"How long's the hike?"

"There's the short way and the long way."

"And we're taking—"

"Whichever way you'd like."

He grinned, and Eve's heart fluttered. For a moment, it was impossible to believe this wasn't a date. A real one, with a guy who was interested in her. But it wasn't, she cautioned herself. Ted was just being gracious, as he likely was to all his brides. "I'd hate to hold up the group."

"No problem in that regard. Once we reach the summit, it will be up to each couple as to how they'd like to head back. There's a steep downhill climb to the boat—which is quicker. Then, a more leisurely stroll down the mountain and around the lake, which is private." He shot her a wink, and Eve's cheeks flamed. "Can't go playing the chaperone at all times. Folks do need a chance to get to know one another."

And make out in nature, Eve thought, her face warming again. She couldn't help but think of Ted and her alone in the wilderness, a cooling breeze rippling off the lake as he held her close, her dress blowing in the wind behind her. Wait! What was she doing wearing a dress on a hike?

"Here's the place!"

Eve noticed he'd paused before the door to an elegant restaurant. A smattering of wrought iron tables were set up on the sidewalk, and a few diners ate by candlelight outdoors. "Hungry?" he asked, leading her inside.

"Famished." Her stomach rumbled, and Eve realized she'd barely eaten all day.

"Excellent. They've got just the thing here to fix you up."

A little while later, they were seated at a cozy table enjoying the selection Ted had recommended, free-range buffalo steak cooked medium rare with fingerling potatoes and braised vegetables. Eve was always up for adventure and enjoyed trying local foods when she traveled. Something about tasting buffalo had sounded wildly exotic. Besides, it was Ted's recommendation, and—at his insistence—he was buying.

When she'd spied the price tag on the expensive bottle of merlot he'd ordered, she was glad. Not that she was flat broke or anything. But being a single girl living on her own in New York meant she had to watch her money, just to ensure the bills got paid and she could still afford groceries. She never would have taken an extravagant trip to Wyoming like this on her own. The fee for participation in Wild West Brides was already in the four figures, and that did *not* include airfare.

"What do you think of the steak?" Ted set down his fork as a waiter stopped by to top off their glasses of wine.

"It's actually quite good. A little gamey but different. I'm glad I tried it."

He raised his glass to hers once the waiter had gone. "Here's to trying new things."

"When they don't involve horses."

He chuckled. "You'll do better next time."

She clinked his glass, her heart feeling light. While she knew she had to get to her confession, she reasoned it could wait until dessert. Why spoil a perfectly delightful meal in the meantime? Eve hadn't enjoyed the company of an attractive man in forever. And Ted was *very* nice looking. It was fun being out with him and seeing other women glance their way with envy. The great thing was, unlike other handsome men she'd known, Ted didn't seem aware of it. He focused all his attention on her.

This had been such a great evening, and their conversation, which started with small talk, had ultimately turned to family. He'd asked about hers and learned that she was an only child. He, on the other hand, admitted to being from a big brood, which included four brothers.

"Are all of you cowboys?" she asked, feeling herself flirt.

He set down his wine. "Oh no."

Eve glanced over her shoulder, trying to track what had startled him. "Ted?" she asked setting her gaze back on his.

He furtively peered behind her, then scooted down in his chair. Way down. If she didn't know better, she'd swear he was trying to hide from somebody.

"Are you all right?"

"I can't believe my eyes!" a stylish blonde proclaimed, striding toward them. The gentleman who accompanied her was tall and bronzed with salt-and-pepper hair.

He studied Ted with alarm. "I must admit this is a surprise."

"Mom... Dad..." Ted choked out the words, then took a swallow of water. "What are you doing in Wyoming?"

The man gave Eve a cursory glance, then fixed his gaze on Ted. "We might ask you the same thing."

Ted's mother surveyed Eve as well, but after a beat, her expression softened. "Well, of course, Bart." She nudged her husband. "They're here together. On vacation. Just like we are."

Eve opened her mouth to speak but shut it.

Bart's voice boomed, causing several heads to swivel in their direction. "Shouldn't you be studying for the bar about now?"

"Bar?" Eve muttered weakly. She didn't mean to comment but couldn't stop herself. What in the world was going on?

Ted blinked at her, his face red from the neck up.

"Why are you wearing that shirt, son?" his mother asked, surveying the chambray plaid. "And how about those boots! Oh my."

"That can't be your hat on the bench beside you," his dad said with obvious disapproval. He clucked his tongue at his wife. "He looks like he's dressed for a rodeo."

Eve tried to intercede. "Ted was just taking me out—"

Ted's dad's eyes flashed at his son. "And what's this Ted business?"

"Yes, Theodore," his mom wanted to know. "What's it all about?"

Eve swallowed hard and clutched her hands together in her lap. Why were Ted's folks so bent out of shape about his appearance? And what was that business about the bar? Eve felt like she'd opened a book and skipped right to the center, missing all the important background information at the start.

Ted steadied his jaw. "I happen to be on a date, if you don't mind. And my name is Ted now. It would be good of you to remember that."

"Well!" His mother huffed and glanced at Eve. "Has *she* inspired you to this...form of anarchy?"

"Let's not jump to conclusions, Lila," her husband warned her. "Maybe she's a colleague? In his law school class?"

"Law school? No." Eve felt the urge to twist up her hair but then realized it was already pinned in place at her nape.

"Eve writes travel brochures for a living, if it's any of your business. Which it isn't."

"Heavens!" Lila paled. "You mean she travels, don't you? You're a travel writer, dear?" she asked, addressing Eve.

Eve grimaced under the weight of her disapproval. "Up until now, it's been more like a desk job. Administrative."

Lila nabbed a small dessert card from the table, fanning herself. "You're a *secretary*?

"What's wrong with being a secretary?" Ted challenged.

That was what Eve had been about to ask, but she'd been too stunned. She'd basically been an AA for her first two years out of school, and there was nothing wrong with her—or that job. She didn't know what was going on here but she was clearly an interloper in this family affair. In a very big way, Eve wanted out. She made a motion to stand, and Ted reached across the table, gently taking her arm.

"Please," he said, pleading. "Stay."

He turned his attention on his parents. "You were a *secretary* once, Mom—to *Dad.*" He gave her a pointed look, and she flushed. His voice had a hard edge to it. "I've been meaning to talk to both of you. But now's not the time."

"Bart," Lila said with a little huff. "They clearly want us to go."

Bart addressed Eve. "I am sorry you got caught up in this. I'm sure it's through no fault of your own."

"Of course it's not," Lila said. "She can't help it that her boyfriend has basically cut off his parents and hasn't spoken to them in months!"

"Boyfriend?"

The older couple stared at her.

"It's all right, Eve," Ted said. "They're going."

Lila's cool gaze fixed on Eve's. "You were saying...?"

Eve's head whirled with confusion. "Ted and I are not *involved.* I'm actually a—"

Ted stopped her. "You don't have to explain yourself. To them or anyone."

"But I want to. Your parents seem to have gotten totally the wrong impression."

Ted pulled a billfold from his pocket and spoke to Eve. "Let's get out of here. I'll make it up to you."

"I think we'd like to hear what the young woman has to say," Bart cut in.

"I was just trying to tell you. Trying to explain. You've got nothing to worry about with me and Ted. I'm not his girlfriend."

"What are you, then?" Lila wanted to know.

Ted held up his hand, but the words flew from her mouth. "One of his brides."

"One?" Bart shouted.

A split second later, Lila fainted against him.

A few hours later, Eve and Ted sat nursing paper cups of coffee on a park bench in the main square. After the scene Ted's parents had created in the restaurant, they hadn't stayed much longer. A frantic waiter had rushed over with a chair for Lila and then returned seconds later with a glass of cold water. This seemed to revive her instantly, so quickly, in fact, that Eve wondered whether the fainting spell had been an act. Ted's parents had joined them at their table while Ted uncomfortably waited on the check, his fingers drumming the table. The silence among the four of them had been so thick one could have cut it with a knife.

Finally, his dad had spoken, just after Ted settled the bill. He'd surveyed his son with red-rimmed eyes, something akin to remorse settled there. "Were you even planning to ask us to the wedding?"

Instead of answering, Ted had stood, then taken Eve by the hand, pulling her to her feet. "I'll talk to the two of you later," he'd said with an agitated scowl before heading for the door.

They seemed to wander aimlessly, dodging nighttime ramblers cluttering the small town's sidewalks. Eve was unsure of what to do or say other than keep Ted company. If he'd wanted to be alone, she figured he'd have said so. After a bit of meandering, he paused by a take-out deli and asked if she wanted some coffee. They'd gotten a few carryout cups and had taken them to the park.

They sat there listening to the night's sounds and the fading commotion of tourists making their way back to their hotels after stepping out for dinner. At long last, Ted broke the silence between them. "I don't know how I can apologize for what went on back there, but I want to."

She studied him in the shadows, the dip of his cowboy hat hiding the emotion in his eyes. "They seemed so surprised to see you."

"Yeah."

"They didn't know? Know you lived in Jackson Hole?"

Ted slowly shook his head. "There's something you don't understand about my family. Everybody has *expectations*. Ideals they're meant to live up to."

"Like going to law school?"

He met her eyes, and this time his emotion was clear. It was like he was fighting something, and as if he'd been waging that battle for a long time. "I always wanted to head out west. Lead my own life. Wide-open spaces, you know?"

She nodded.

"The place I come from. That *life*. It was always so confining."

"You're not from Wyoming, are you?"

He removed his hat and ran his fingers through his hair. "Boston."

Eve drew a sharp breath.

"My dad's family was in shipping. For generations back. They built an empire, thanks to the efforts of their Ivy League sons and daughters."

"I don't suppose being a cowboy fit the bill."

"No. Going to law school did. Or medical school at least. Three of my brothers are doctors. The rogue one is a public defender."

Eve stifled a giggle. "That's radical."

He met her gaze with all seriousness. "In my family, it is."

Worry lines creased his eyes, and she fought the temptation to reach out and touch him. "You're a grown man, Ted."

"Yeah, I know it. Just try to tell it to the two of them."

He leaned back on the bench and stretched one arm behind her on the seat back. The breeze picked up, and Eve buttoned the sweater she'd slipped on earlier. Ted pursed his lips, surveying her. "Too chilly for you?"

"I'm fine," she told him honestly. "The coffee warms me up." She took another sip, gathering her nerve. "It's hard keeping secrets."

"What do you mean?"

"Pretending to be who you're not."

Ted surprised her with a chuckle. "I'm not really pretending. What you see here?" He thumbed his chest. "Is the real McCoy. I don't need to have been born here to understand that. This is where I'm meant to be."

"And what you're meant to do," she added.

"Yes."

"You seem mighty sure of that."

"That's because I am. I spent a long time thinking about it. Brian and I prepared for everything. Wild West Brides isn't some fly-by-night operation. It was well thought out, meticulously planned. Right down to those algorithms."

"The ones that never fail."

His gaze locked on hers, and Eve's breath caught in her throat. He seemed to be studying her in a way, discerning something. "They've never failed before."

She pushed the words out and whispered, "Maybe they failed for a reason."

There was heat in his eyes, heat and longing too. Ted trailed a finger down her cheek. "I'm starting to think I know that reason."

He was nearer now, closing the distance between them. Eve's heart lurched, and she feared he might do something crazy, like grab her and kiss her. Then she found herself wishing he would.

"The reason…" Her voice squeaked. "The reason they failed is because I didn't fill out those forms."

"You what?" He stared at her in surprise. "Why?"

She tried to keep her voice strong, but it came out as a whimper. "You're not the only one who's been lying about who you are."

Chapter Twelve

Ted massaged his forehead, then set his hat back on his head. "I don't understand why you didn't just call up and arrange an interview."

"Ross said it would be better this way."

"Well, Ross was wrong. This way got somebody hurt."

Her cheeks colored slightly. "You don't know how awful I feel about that."

And for the life of him, he believed her. Eve didn't seem like the sort of woman who liked to hurt people. Ted had met that kind before and had vowed to steer clear of them. He shook his head, thinking. If it wasn't Eve's information in the profile but someone else's, that meant the other person might be a match for Scott. Then again, that other person had submitted information under false pretenses, not exactly the sort of clientele Ted endorsed. He decided to push the whole notion aside, letting sleeping dogs lie. Once this week was through and his decks were cleared, he'd get in touch with Scott and offer a full refund. It was the least he could do.

"I wouldn't blame you if you wanted to kick me out of the group." Eve hung her head. "If you want me to go now, I will."

"What about your story?"

"I don't even know if I want to write it anymore."

"Eve?"

When she looked up at him, her eyes were moist. "This was supposed to be my big chance, you know. An opportunity to break out of copyediting and into full-fledged reporting."

He met her gaze and held it. "That chance isn't over, as far as I can tell."

She blinked, not understanding.

"Eve, listen to me. I'm the last one here who should be casting any stones about fake identities."

"But you said—"

"I know what I said about Scott. I'm still sorry about that too. Sorry there had to be some fallout from your deception. But I'm planning to make things right with Scott. I'll give him back his money. All of it."

"Will that be enough?"

"It will have to be, for now."

"What are you saying, Ted? That you want me to stay for the rest of the week?"

"I'm telling you two things. One, that I want you to stay." His heart thumped and then beat louder. "And two, that you can still do your story."

Her face brightened. "Really?"

"Ask me anything you want! I'm an open book."

She eyed him sheepishly. "It's okay, then? Okay if I stick around, pretend that I'm part of the group?"

"Well…" He drew out the word. "No. We can't have that exactly."

"What do you mean?"

"If you stay on with Wild West Brides, you'll have to come clean. Tell the other couples what you're up to and ask if they mind being included in your article."

"But I wouldn't use—"

"Even if the names are changed to protect the innocent."

Her cheeks turned a dusty rose. "How did you know what I was about to say?"

"I was training to be a lawyer, remember? I'm good at putting words in other people's mouths."

"How long were you in law school?"

"A year and a half was all I could take. All those hours spent poring over tomes, when all I could think of was being in the great outdoors."

Eve settled back on the bench, satisfied with his answers. It felt good telling Ted the truth, and she'd appreciated hearing his story too. Suddenly there was a new closeness between them, as if barriers and pretenses had been dropped. And since they were buds now, she figured she might as well ask. Eve blew out a small breath, then spoke quietly. "What are you going to do about your parents?"

He tipped his hat toward her and shook his head. "Honestly? I have no idea."

They discussed Ted's options all the way back to Eve's hotel. A, he could confront his parents and ask them to butt out of his life, which neither of them thought was the right idea. Or B, he could try to make peace and explain how their failure to accept his personal choices had been a disappointment. Of course, they didn't exactly understand they'd failed to support him, because up until now both Bart and Lila still believed Ted to be in law school in California. Perhaps he'd been wrong not to tell them the truth, but Ted confessed he'd grown so weary of battling his parents at every turn, he'd decided to step outside the box and chart his own course. "Just do it, you know?"

"I think I understand what you're saying," Eve told him. "You couldn't take any more resistance."

"I knew what they would have said if I'd told them of my plans to launch Wild West Brides. They would have asked me if I was out of my mind."

"So, you thought cutting them off was the solution?" While Lila and Bart hadn't particularly impressed Eve, she was a big believer in family. And family stuck together, most of the time. At least that was what she'd grown up believing in her single-parent home. It had just been her and her dad, but he'd been there for her. Rock solid.

"I never intended it to be permanent," he informed her. "I was just waiting for things to settle here. Once the business was going strong—"

"But it *is* going strong, isn't it?"

His face brightened in a smile. "It's going dynamite. I can't wait to tell you all about it. For your article."

"Then, why haven't you...? About your mom and dad...?"

"I'd planned to tell them at Thanksgiving. We Walkers all go home for the holiday. It's great fun to see my brothers and their wives, and I love playing with my nieces and nephews."

"All married?"

"I'm the lone holdout, yup."

Eve glanced at him, and his skin burned.

"Anyway, my point is, I always intended to tell them. I wasn't putting it off entirely. Just long enough to get established in my new business, so they'd know there was no way to talk me out of it."

"You've had no communication with them in all this time?" she asked with disbelief.

"I had my mail forwarded here from school. I've phoned and e-mailed a couple of times, but never got into any conversations that were long-winded."

"You were waiting for the right time."

"Yes."

"It *is* your life, Ted."

"I know. That's why I'm trying to lead it. Independently."

"No strings? No one to tie you down?"

He eyed her curiously.

"Are we still talking about my parents or something else?"

Her face flushed. "I was just wondering why... I mean, how it is you play matchmaker to so many people but haven't found a match of your own?"

"Is that a professional question, or is it personal?"

She adjusted the clip in her hair. "Maybe both."

Ted stared up at the darkened sky, his gaze lingering a moment, then set his eyes back on hers. "There was someone a while ago. When I was in law school."

"What happened?"

"All she wanted was a meal ticket."

"I'm sorry."

"It's all right, Eve. You asked, so I'm telling you. Just please don't print this in your article."

"I wouldn't dare... Would never do that." She laid a hand on his arm as they reached the hotel. "I appreciate that you've told me things. That you've opened up to me. And I want you to know that what we say between us, as..." She fumbled for the word, so he filled in.

"Friends?"

She heaved a sigh and smiled. "Yes, friends. What I'm trying to say is anything we discuss as friends is just between us. That's how it should be and how I want it to stay."

"Thanks." Ted adjusted his hat. "And about law school..."

"I really shouldn't have asked."

"It's water under the bridge."

"Everyone needs someone to see them for who they really are."

"Yes." Ted took a step toward her, and electricity sparked between them. "How about you?" he asked quietly. "Have you found someone like that? Someone who sees you for who you are?" She slowly gazed up at him, and their eyes locked in a heated trance. When she failed to answer, he lowered his chin and whispered, "Ever come close?"

Eve licked her lips, and he burned to claim her mouth with his.

She whispered back, barely breathing the words, "Always a bridesmaid."

His mouth was so close she could feel his breath on her lips.

"That's a damn shame. But not for your groom."

She was yearning, aching for his kiss.

"What groom?"

"The one who's going to marry you someday." Dark eyes danced. "Wild West Bride."

Eve felt like the earth had moved beneath her, setting her world off-kilter. What had just happened here with that almost, near-kiss?

"Now you're teasing me." She huffed, upset.

Ted cupped her cheek with his hand. "No."

"No, what?"

"I'm only fooling myself." His gazed deepened, and the look spoke volumes. "You don't know how much I want to kiss you."

"But you won't."

"I have a business to run."

"I'm not a part of your business."

He took her in his arms, and Eve swooned. His eyes were passionate, predatory.

"I'd like to make you my business."

"Ted..."

He tightened his embrace, his voice husky. "Tell me to walk away, and I will."

But she couldn't. Simply couldn't say no, especially when he was this close, close enough to... She found her mouth tilting up toward his, her lips parting slightly. Then his heat was upon her, and she lost her bearings. His rough kiss consumed her with masculine desire. The kind she'd envisioned in her dreams. Her pulse pounded furiously as her body cried out for more. More kissing. More Ted. *More cowboy.*

He held her close, and Eve wound her arms around him, upsetting the hat from his head and knocking it skyward as he devoured her with hot, hungry kisses again and again. She sighed up against him, her breasts molded to his rock-hard chest, her knees threatening to give way. She'd never been kissed like this. Not in her entire life.

"Oh my."

Ted gently broke their embrace, steadying her in one strong arm. There was a sexy gleam in his eye when he spoke. "I'll take that as a compliment."

Eve's heart beat wildly, and her head spun. "Ted," she gasped. "I... We..." She wanted to protest, say they shouldn't have done that. But that would be a lie.

"We can try it again tomorrow," he said with a sexy wink. "Up at Jenny Lake. We'll take the long way back."

Ted stooped low for a second to scoop something off the ground. When he handed it over, Eve saw it was the clip that had become dislodged from her hair. All at once, Eve became aware of the waves that had spilled to her shoulders, the heat in her belly, and the fire at the back of her neck.

"You look beautiful." He strummed her cheek with the back of his hand, his touch igniting her skin.

"You look pretty good yourself." She was still out of breath, panting from their heady exchange.

"Forgive me?" he asked with an earnest look.

"For what?"

A sly smile crept across his lips. "For not being able to resist you. I've never done that before, you know. Not with any of my clients, ever."

"I hope not," she said, aching to fall back into his arms. Eve was so turned around, she didn't know what to think or do. One thing she knew for sure, falling for some guy in Wyoming was not on her agenda. And boy, was she falling fast.

"I'll see you tomorrow." He leaned forward and gave her a chaste peck on the lips. "Until then," he said, his voice husky, "I'll be thinking of you all night through."

That makes two of us, Eve thought with a sigh.

Before he released her, he met her eyes with a serious stare. "I have something to ask you. A favor... Tomorrow, in front of the group. Could you not blow my cover?"

"You want me to come clean, but not you?"

"This is a little different, Eve. The whole cowboy thing. It's part of my shtick. The rough-and-tough cowboy behind Wild West Brides. It makes it more fun for everyone. You know?"

Lila scooted back around the corner, tugging Bart with her. "Did you see that?"

"That almost looked like our boy," Bart confided.

"Our boy with that new bride of his," Lila said with a sniff.

"You don't think they're married yet?"

"I didn't see any wedding rings."

Bart studied his wife with surprise. "You checked?"

"Women always check." She huffed. "I can't believe he didn't tell us."

"About what?"

"The engagement!"

Bart set his jaw in a frown. "Just think, if we hadn't come here on this golfing conference—"

She waved the thought away. "What matters now is that we *are* here, and our Theodore is obviously getting married."

"Didn't the girl say there were others involved?"

"Heavens, Bart! I'm sure we misheard her. This isn't Salt Lake City."

Bart peered around the corner as Eve slipped into her hotel. "You're right, we probably misunderstood. *One* of her seems like plenty to handle. Did you see how she nearly tackled him? Right there on the sidewalk?"

"From my perspective it looked mutual." Lila twisted her lips, then glanced at Bart. "It also looked serious."

"Indeed."

"Maybe we should get to know her?"

"How? Theodore doesn't even want us around!"

An SUV drove past them, then turned right at the intersection. Lila's mouth dropped open. "Did you see that? Wyoming tags!"

"So?"

"That was our son driving!"

Bart glanced at his wife. "Something's not adding up here."

"Maybe he rented it?"

Lila stared at him flatly.

"Okay, okay." He stroked his sturdy chin, considering. "I'll ask around at the club, see what folks know."

Lila frowned. "That boy never wanted to go to law school."

"I can't imagine he'd drop out and not tell us."

"And that he'd moved to Wyoming!"

"You think he did it for that girl?"

"She's the one in a hotel!" Lila pointed out.

"Hmm. You're right," Bart agreed. "Maybe she's moving here for him."

"Imagine! But, why?"

Bart shook his head. "It has to be something big. Something life changing."

"But *marriage*! It's such a big step."

"Theodore wouldn't do that unless he was sure."

"Well, he's sure rushing into it," Lila replied.

Their eyes traveled back toward Eve's hotel.

Bart's eyes lit with understanding. "You don't think that she's...?"

They stopped and gaped at each other.

Lila leapt into her husband's arms and squealed with delight. "We're going to be grandparents!"

Ted stared in his rearview mirror, thinking he couldn't have seen that right. Some tourist couple on the corner was staring and pointing at his departing SUV. Hold on. The woman was blonde, middle-aged, and looked a whole heck of a lot like... Suddenly, his dad's distant gaze was upon him, and Ted lowered the gas pedal to the floor, high-tailing it out of town. Thank goodness he'd passed the last traffic light and had made it to the open highway, where he could pick up speed without breaking any laws.

Sooner or later, he'd have to hunt down his parents and set things straight. But for now, Ted needed to focus on tomorrow. He was leading another Wild West Brides adventure, and he looked forward to this one more than ever. Eve would be coming along, and he'd make plans to ensure she had a really great time.

He didn't know what had happened back at her hotel, but neither of them had been able to stop themselves. And maybe that was okay. What was wrong with a little mutual attraction on a warm summer night? Ted's heart sank. Everything. He had no business leading Eve on by getting involved with her. She was here to write an article, and had cleared that part up. And Ted...? Well, Ted was just here to do his job as he always had. Set his mind to matchmaking and ensure that all the couples had a good time.

Yeah, right, he thought with a frown in the mirror. All the couples but him. That's how it always was, and why? Was it because Ted had been too gun-shy to get back out there on his own? Is that why he'd convinced himself he wasn't looking?

Ted clearly hadn't been looking when Eve came into the picture, and he certainly hadn't planned to start falling for her when she'd done those gymnastics on her horse. But she'd captured him in that moment with her wacky, irreverent charm. And that had been just the beginning. He'd been drawn to her ever since but had been determined to fight it.

Once Scott was gone, it was even tougher to keep his resolve. Before his parents torpedoed their dinner, they'd been having a fantastic time. Even afterward, and in spite of the family drama, the way they'd talked together had seemed so easy. In just one evening, he'd told her things about himself and about his life that he'd barely told anyone else. It was impossible not to notice her looks, or the sexy way those auburn curls played about her pretty face. And when her big dark eyes stared at him, his heart skipped a beat.

Her introduction to his parents had been a baptism by fire, but she'd handled it all with reasonable aplomb, despite the fact they'd been incredibly rude to her. When he'd explained more about the situation later, she'd been kind and understanding. Not judgmental, the way a certain ex might have been.

Ted shook his head, trying to ward off the feel of Eve's warm and welcoming kiss. But she'd branded him all the same. He wished now he'd never taken her in his arms, because all it left him wanting to do was hold her again— and soon. If he played his cards right, perhaps he'd have that opportunity tomorrow.

Chapter Thirteen

They rolled out of town, and the vast landscape opened up before them, reminding Eve of the view she'd encountered when she'd first stepped off the plane. Jackson Hole airport was a quaint little fly station with high wood beams, and large plate glass windows framing the Teton Mountains. The majesty of the range was impressive as it clawed at the sky with jagged peaks, tipped white like snowy talons.

While the modest runways were serviceable for aircraft, the place somehow had the feel of an old stagecoach stop, or perhaps somewhere that had once been a faraway outpost on a pioneer railway. Yet there was beauty in the isolation. Rolling meadows stretched wide, caught up in the shadows of the mountains and towering clouds that blocked the sun from time to time during its morning ascent. They were passing the airport now. Eve watched as a small plane touched down, its wheels grazing the tarmac.

She could imagine what its passengers were thinking, especially the ones who'd never been to Jackson Hole. They were bound to believe they'd been transported into some fanciful fantasyland. To someplace you might see in a high-end science fiction movie. She knew because that was how she'd felt herself.

"Only airport in a national park," Brian informed the group. He sat behind the wheel with Ted riding shotgun beside him. Without needing to discuss why, Eve and Ted had kept things purposely casual when they'd greeted each other among the others in Eve's hotel lobby. He'd given her a brief good morning, and she'd returned a subtle

"Hey." But a silent signal had flashed between them just the same. A signal saying things would be much less casual when they were all alone.

"It's breathtaking," Gayle said. "I couldn't believe my eyes when I landed here."

"I know, right?" Stephen said, snuggling her under his arm. Eve sat on Gayle's other side, feeling like a third wheel nestled next to the lovebirds on the middle bench. She glanced over her shoulder, thinking things wouldn't have been any better in back. Danni and Chet looked awfully cozy too. No way! They were Eskimo kissing and making baby-talk noises. A sour taste rose in Eve's throat, and she fumbled in her purse for some gum. And there she'd thought Danni would be the tough one. That just showed how much she knew about Wild West Brides. Which reminded her...

Gayle turned her way. "We were really sorry to hear about Scott's daughter, Eve. Know you must be bummed to be left here all alone."

"She's not alone," Ted piped in from up front.

Brian briefly swiveled his head with a grin. "Ted's filling in."

Danni was suddenly at attention. "Oooh," she said exaggerating the word. "How nice!"

Eve's cheeks warmed. "Oh no, it's not like—"

"It's all right," Gayle said with a giggle. "We're sure Ted's due for a little R&R."

Brian stifled a chuckle, and Ted shot him a look.

Stephen leaned forward to pat Ted's shoulder. "Looks like the Wild West cowboy might get a bride of his own."

Ted choked on his water, and Brian grabbed the bottle away and set it in its holder.

"What about you, Brian?" Gayle asked with interest. "Got anyone special?"

"The old man's practically married," Ted answered.

Brian smiled into the rearview mirror. "Sorry, ladies. I hate to disappoint you, but it's true."

"*I'm* happy enough," Danni said, snuggling up to Chet.

"That makes four of us!" Gayle's guy said.

Ted spun in his seat to address them. "Speaking of happy couples!" He clapped his hands together. "Eve here has something to tell you."

Eve felt the heat at the back of her neck and twisted up her ponytail, securing the ends of it in a lump beneath the elastic band. "That's right."

Suddenly, all eyes were on her.

"The truth is, I... What I'm saying is—"

"Spill it, sister," Gayle encouraged in a monotone.

"She's a reporter," Ted said, after a pause where Eve apparently couldn't answer.

"Wow." Brian twisted his lips and considered this. "That's pretty cool."

Danni sat up in her seat. "From someplace famous?"

"*Make It Count* magazine," Eve admitted.

"I've heard of it!" Danni appeared pleased, but Gayle was nonplussed.

"I haven't."

"Maybe that's because all you read are environmental journals," her partner told her.

She flushed under his admiring gaze. "Too true."

"So what's this mean?" Chet asked. "That we're on *Candid Camera?*"

Ted raised a cautionary hand. "Only if you want to be."

"I'm here to do a piece," Eve explained rapidly, "on Ted Walker and his business."

Gayle eyed her astutely. "So *that's* your interest in him."

Danni snapped her fingers in back. "Still *could be* romantic!"

"Who knew my little muffin would have such a heart of gold," her man said. Ted stared over his shoulder at Eve, who mouthed back to him, *little muffin?*

"So, you don't mind?" Ted asked them. "You're all right with Eve doing her story?"

"If you want to conceal your identities, I'm perfectly cool with that," Eve said. "I can supply false names or not even mention you at all."

The two men looked doubtful, while Gayle pursed her lips. "I'll have to think about it," she finally said.

"Take all the time you need," Eve answered. "Meanwhile, I'll just focus on Ted."

Did Eve imagine it, or did the back of his neck deepen a hue above the neckline of his T-shirt?

Danni frowned and sat back in her seat. "I don't mind giving you my story. Even if Chet won't supply his end of it."

"I didn't say I wouldn't," he chimed in.

"You will?" she asked, delighted.

"If it's okay with you, it's fine by me."

She beamed at him, then gave Eve a thumbs-up. "Look!" she shouted, pointing out the window. "More buffalo!"

Eve turned her gaze on the field beside them. It was dotted by tiny dark figures that—wait! "Oh my gosh!" she cried, excited. "They're for real?" Herds of them were grazing, their prominent hunched backs cutting a swath across the landscape like shadowbox silhouettes. Tourists had pulled off at overlooks to gawk and take photos, their children scrambling high on split-rail fences to get a better look. Some held binoculars.

Ted reached into the glove box and pulled out his own pair, handing them to Eve. "Care to stop and take a look?"

She nodded eagerly and they pulled off at a designated area. When she stepped from the SUV with the others, Eve saw the animals were even larger than she'd imagined. Eve recalled seeing one on an old buffalo nickel ages ago. Her uncle had collected coins and showed her one when she was still in grade school. Eve had thought of the bison like a mythical creature. Not quite a steer and not quite an ox, but something all its own. Something unique and historic that defied all explanation. And she'd eaten one of them just last night. Eve's stomach heaved, and she gripped it, lowering the binoculars.

"What's wrong?" Ted asked from beside her.

"Buffalo steak," she said, pushing the meaty memory aside and trying to focus instead on the delicate garlic flavoring on fingerling potatoes.

Ted bellowed a laugh and brought his arm around her. "Don't tell me you have this reaction to dairy farms?"

Eve felt flushed and lightheaded, staring at the poor, meandering beasts. "We don't have many of those in New York City."

Ted gave her shoulder a little squeeze, then released it as he noticed the others looking on. "Come on," he said with a whisper. "I've got some antacids in my pack."

She eyed him gratefully. "You keep them for emergencies?"

His lips crept into a grin. "I keep them for tourists."

"Thanks a lot." She hobbled toward the SUV, with Ted helping her. "I'll take two," she whispered back.

The hike to the falls was amazing. They rode a ferry across the pristine lake where the reflection of mountains shimmered in the glistening waters. On the other side, they found a footpath that wound up around a rocky ledge, and then another…climbing higher to the top. When they finally reached their high plateau, Ted pointed to the vista below them. Mountains ringed the lake as the sound of splashing waters gurgled above.

"Where are the falls?"

Ted met her eyes, and sunshine glimmered in his. "Not much farther."

Eve clutched her side and heaved in breaths. Though she was reasonably fit, her body wasn't used to the effort of the climb, especially at this altitude.

"Everyone okay to go on?" Brian cast her a wary glance, then addressed the group. The others nodded their assent and followed after him, but Ted caught Eve's hand when she trailed behind them.

"Stay with me. Take a breather."

Eve flushed to think she was slowing the group down. "I don't want to be the heavyweight."

"Who said anything about heavy?" Ted drew his arms around her and pulled her close. A family who'd also been admiring the view had just departed, leaving them alone. Ted grinned, and her pulse fluttered. "At the moment, I couldn't feel any lighter."

"Ted…"

He brought his mouth to hers as a warm breeze combed her hair. "You're not mad at me, are you?" He whispered the words that brushed against her lips. "Mad that I'm not a real cowboy?"

Eve's heart hammered harder. "You're as real as any I've known."

He chuckled, then pressed his lips to hers. Once…twice..three times. "How many…have there…been?" he asked between kisses.

Eve heard herself whimper. "One," she said, holding him close.

"Then I'd better not mess this up." Ted deepened his kiss as winds rippled around them. Eve's cheeks flamed and her breasts warmed as she molded up against him. She'd certainly never been kissed like this. Oh yes, she had. Last night.

They heard footsteps approaching on the gravel path and broke apart. Ted cupped her chin and gently stroked her cheek with his thumb. "We'll have more time alone later."

Eve was still dizzy from the taste of him when he took her hand. "Come on, I want you to see the falls."

When they reached the base of the tumbling waters, the others in their group had already broken out their lunches. Ted had told them all to pack sandwiches and fill large water bottles. Eve took a grateful swig from hers, then studied their surroundings. "It's beautiful." The cascading waters kicked up a soft spray, spritzing them with cool droplets. Nobody tried to move away. After the long trek up the mountain, the soothing sprinkles felt good.

Ted pretended to admire the falls, but Eve sensed his eyes were on her. "Very few sights can compare."

Brian munched on his sub roll before addressing the couples. "Any hardy types want to hike back?"

Danni removed a sneaker and rubbed her sore instep. "I'll take the boat, if that's all right."

"I think I'd like that too," Gayle agreed.

Their dates looked at each other, then spoke almost at once. "We'll go with them."

Ted raised his eyebrows at Eve. The truth was, she was dead tired but believed she could rally for a bit more alone time with her cowboy. She was sure she could convince him to take it slow. "I'm up for whatever you are."

Danni narrowed her eyes. "Mm-hm."

"What's that mean?" Eve asked her.

"Oh…nothing!" the blonde chirped cheerily. "Nothing at all."

Gayle whispered behind her hand, but Eve heard her. "Looks like Scott's been replaced."

Brian started strapping on his pack. "Ready to move out?"

"In just a second," Stephen added.

"No hurries," Ted offered congenially. "Everyone stay and enjoy the view as long as you'd like." Then he shot a wink at Eve when the others weren't looking.

She blushed and dropped her chin, pretending to focus on the turkey club she'd bought from the deli by her hotel. "Always loved dining al fresco!" she said, taking a bite.

Ted settled down beside her on a large flat-topped boulder. "And I always liked long walks after lunch," he whispered when the rest were distracted.

"You really are one terrible flirt!" Eve scolded as they made their way down the mountain. Ted had led them to a smaller path at the foot of the hills that wrapped around the lake.

"Who says I was flirting?" He glanced over his shoulder with a serious look, but mirth danced in his eyes.

"I do!"

"That wasn't flirting!"

"No?" Why was he walking so fast? She was growing breathless trying to catch up! Wasn't this supposed to be a romantic stroll? Something more leisurely paced? "Won't you slow down?"

He kept trudging ahead, parting foliage with his hands as he went. "In just a second."

"Why? Where are we going?"

Ted held back a nest of branches with one arm and stepped aside, exposing the breathtaking vista. "Here."

"Oh my."

He held out a free hand, and Eve took it as he led her up to the crest of a rocky ledge. She stared out at the sunlight dancing across the stunning panorama encompassing the mountains and the lake. There wasn't another soul in sight. "It's gorgeous. It's almost like someone created it just for the two of us."

"I know." Ted released the branches, and suddenly they were shielded in their own private space, with trees at their backs and a huge open sky above. His deep brown eyes were sultry, swimming with emotion. "Okay, I'll admit it." His voice rumbled low and sexy. "I was flirting back there. A little."

"A *lot*," she teased, moving closer.

He took her in his arms. "Watch your step."

"Too late for that."

"Yeah." He gave her a kiss. "I know what you mean."

"Ted?" she asked him. "What are you going to do about your parents?"

"Talk to them, I guess."

"When?"

"Some time after our rafting trip."

Eve swallowed hard. "Whose rafting trip?"

Ted chuckled and jostled her in his arms. "You really didn't read that brochure, did you?"

"I, uh…"

He trapped her in his gaze.

"Nope."

"But you will come?" He read her doubtful look. "I really wish you would. It would mean a lot to me."

"As the director of Wild West Brides?"

"No, as something else."

Eve's heart thumped.

"Your cowboy." A slow smile spread across his lips. "You make me feel like I am one, you know. Like I'm the real thing."

"Maybe that's because you are."

"I'm not roping steer or riding the range."

"You run Sunnyvale Ranch."

He grinned warmly. "That's something."

"It fits you, Ted. *This* fits you. Making other people happy fits you."

He surveyed her with a deep longing. "Are you happy, Eve?"

She thought about this for the first time. The truth was, when she'd come to Wyoming, she'd been miserable. Now, in just a few short days, her mood had morphed into something else. It was like her life was no longer a dead end. The whole world held possibilities. Maybe this was what came of spending time outdoors. Or perhaps it was just the heady appeal of being wrapped in Ted's arms. "I am," she told him surely. She shot him a warming smile. "Very happy. Who knew I was such a nature girl?"

His voice grew husky. "Who knew?"

"Aren't the others going to miss us?"

"The ranger station has a really great gift shop."

"How big?" she asked.

"Enormous. Huge. They could browse there for hours."

"Oh, Ted," she said, sighing into him.

He guided her gently toward the ground. "Do me a favor… Don't write this in your story." There was a small clearing between the trees and the water, where the earth was cushioned by springy moss and grass.

She let him cradle her in his arms and lay her on the bed that nature had laid beneath them. He kissed her and eased down beside her, tenderly stroking her hair. "We can head back if you want to." But the look in his eyes said Ted didn't want to go anywhere but here. All he wanted was Eve, and he had to have her right now. Eve's temperature spiked as she recalled the fiery heat of Ted's kisses and the rock-hard press of his body.

"I don't want to head back," she said, feeling her face flush. The rest of her was warming too, from her head down to her toes. "Not yet."

He rolled on top of her and brought his mouth to hers. "I'm glad."

Chapter Fourteen

The minute Eve entered her hotel room, her cell started ringing. She checked it and saw she had several missed calls from Glenn. Only they were just now coming through. Her carrier must not have gotten reception up at the lake.

"Where have you *been* all day?"

Eve dropped her daypack onto the bed. "Up at Jenny Lake. You've got my itinerary. You should know."

"The lake. Right, right. Got it." She could just see him checking off his mental list. "So, the safari was yesterday?"

"Yeah, but I didn't make it."

"Bite your tongue!"

"What?"

"You're on speaker. Ross is in the next room. Hang on, let me take you off."

He pressed a button, and his voice no longer sounded like it was coming from a well. "What do you mean, you didn't make it?" he whispered into the phone. "You're supposed to be covering things."

"I *am* covering things." Eve recalled Ted's body covering hers and her cheeks warmed. "I just wasn't feeling well yesterday, that's all."

"Are you coming down with something?"

Yeah, Eve thought, *a bad case of cowboy.* She and Ted had lingered in the wilderness longer than they should have, yet when they'd met up with the others, it was like they'd barely noticed she and Ted had been gone. Brian had apparently informed them the footpath was the long way around. The rest of the party had amused themselves touring the interesting gift shop, then had settled down to share a bottle of regional chardonnay on some rockers on its front porch.

Glenn cleared his throat at the other end of the line. "I asked if you're getting sick?"

"No, nothing like that," Eve said quickly. She sat heavily on a chair, then kicked off her hiking shoes one at a time. "I was just a little sore from horseback riding."

"Ah."

"I nearly got thrown, Glenn."

"You're blaming me, aren't you?"

"No, I…" Eve pulled the clip from her hair and let it spill to her shoulders. She'd worn it up all day—except for during that brief moment on the ground. Okay, it was more than a brief moment. More like a heavenly out-of-body experience. She'd certainly never experienced a body like Ted's.

Glenn's voice rose. "Are you even hearing me?"

"Of course I am!" Eve returned, a little louder than intended.

"Well, good, because I can't hold Ross off much longer."

"Ross?" Eve asked, surprised.

Glenn heaved a frustrated breath. "Ross wants your first draft—tomorrow."

"*Tomorrow?* That's impossible. The week's not even through!"

"So? Are you getting to know Ted?"

Eve felt herself blush. "A little."

"And you've infiltrated Wild West Brides?"

"Actually, about that—"

"You *are* playing the role, Eve?"

She straightened her spine against the back of the chair. "I'm getting the information as promised."

"Then you should be able to rough something out. Let us know where you're headed."

If only she knew that herself. Somehow things were getting awfully turned around. Eve had come here to write a story, but suddenly she found herself losing her heart. She stared out the window as dusk settled in, realizing it was true. She'd gotten in over her head in Jackson Hole. Way over. She'd mixed business with pleasure, and now who knew if there'd ever be a way to untangle the two.

One thing was certain, no matter the feelings she was developing for Ted, she had to find a way to set her professional goals back on track. She hadn't paid her own way to Wyoming. Her magazine had. She'd been sent here on a very specific mission. Eve still had a job to do, and Ted was okay with that. She'd have to get to her story in earnest ASAP. She'd figure out whatever it was that was going on between her and Ted later.

Ted stepped into the shower, running the water extra hot. Maybe this was a bad idea, he thought, looking down. All that warmth only made him think of Eve. He reluctantly reached for the knob and cooled the shower's stream until his body began to behave. What a great couples' coordinator he was. Coordinating himself right into luscious Eve's arms. *Damn.* He adjusted the shower knob further until the water ran ice-cold. There! He deserved that. Ted lathered his hair, soaped up, and rinsed off, shutting the shower off lickety-split.

He toweled off quickly, thinking he should have known better. *What was I thinking? I've never done anything like that before.* Well, okay, maybe he had. But certainly never in the line of duty. And clearly, never with one of his Wild West Brides! It wasn't like he'd intended things to go that far. He'd thought maybe they'd make out a little. Sneak in a few private kisses… The fact that he'd stashed condoms in his pocket attested more to his optimism than to what he'd believed would actually develop between them.

Ted wrapped a towel around his waist, shaking his head. That's just how things were with Eve, and there was no escaping it. One lingering kiss led to the next, and then another one. And, after a while, kissing couldn't be enough. It would never be enough. Ted wanted all of her. *Well, I'll be*… Ted gritted his teeth and strode back to the bathroom, the towel around his waist gripped tightly with one hand. He used the other to reach in the shower and turn the water back on. Ice-cold.

He had to get a grip. Losing his head over one of his clients wouldn't do. All right, so maybe she wasn't really one of his clients. She was here to do a job and had explained all that. So, what was Ted's role here? Spinning all out of control every time she batted those gorgeous brown eyes? He was drawn to her, he'd admit it. Eve was funny and pretty and incredibly easy to talk to. She was also unbelievably easy to kiss. It was almost as if her lips had been invented just for his, as if all of her had. They'd fit together so perfectly.

Ted sighed heavily as the frigid water streamed down. Tomorrow, he had an adventure to lead. He'd talk to her afterward. He knew he had to give her information for her story. But the next order of business would involve learning what she thought of him—on a personal level.

Ted couldn't bear to believe she was playing him. Only using him for her article. But he'd been used before and was well aware—much more painfully than many men—that sort of thing happened. Ted thought of his parents' disapproval, and of his former girlfriend, then suddenly there was no need for the shower. He shut off the water, toweled dry, and sulked into the next room.

Those were two dour thoughts when coupled together. Memories of Rebecca and the awareness that his parents were still in town. He needed to deal with them soon. Brian had learned they were staying at the club, as Ted suspected. It would be easy to track them down.

Ted sighed heavily, glad at least that the other couples signed on for the week were getting along. Despite complications, things wouldn't be a total bust. In fact, Brian would call them a raging success. He'd likely dismiss Eve and Scott's situation as not counting in the statistics. And maybe they shouldn't, given that Eve had falsified her information anyway. Ted puzzled over why someone like Eve would do that. Now that he'd gotten to know her a bit, that didn't seem like her at all.

Ted was sure there was more to her story, and he was determined to learn all about it. Tomorrow. Ted wearily made for his bed. For now, he needed to forget all about exes, his parents—and the sexy redhead who drove him out of his mind—and get some rest.

Chapter Fifteen

Eve clicked the button on her e-reader, flipping to the final page. *Ten Tips on Turning His Head* didn't offer much in the way of useful advice. It was all about office romance, or flirtation in the big city. Wearing sexy stilettos out here didn't seem very practical. Besides, Ted appeared to like his women a little more on the natural side. Eve's whole body heated as she thought about how *natural* she and Ted had been. Right down to shedding every stitch of clothing in their secret shelter behind the trees.

Her cell buzzed, and she checked it.

Still awake?

It was Ted. Eve quickly answered that she was, then he asked if he could call her. A few seconds later, her phone rang.

"You sure I didn't wake you?" He spoke low and husky, almost like he'd barely awakened himself.

"No, I was reading."

"Oh yeah? What?" She thought she heard the tinkle of ice in the background and imagined him sitting somewhere drinking a shot of whiskey. On the rocks.

Eve glanced at her e-reader, not daring to admit it. "Just some boring old stuff. Research for work."

"Sounds terrible."

"Could be better." Eve ran a hand through her hair. "So, what are you up to?"

He paused a moment, then answered in a wistful way. "Just sitting on my deck. Stargazing."

Eve could only imagine how brilliant the stars must look out there. "Sounds lovely."

"Actually…" His voice dropped a notch. "It's lonely."

"Lonely?"

"I've been thinking about you, Eve. Ever since... What I mean is... Today, at Jenny Lake. Are you okay with what happened?"

She drew a breath, her heart pounding. "I wanted it to happen as much as you did."

"That's what I thought. But I needed to make sure I didn't take advantage—"

"Of me, Ted? I'm a grown woman."

"Of the situation, I meant. The fresh air... The sunshine..."

"The mountains reflecting on the lake." Eve sighed into the receiver. "It was perfect in every way."

"I thought so too."

A stillness fell on the line between them.

After a beat, he said, "I need to see you. *I'd like to*, if I can."

She checked the clock. It was after eleven.

He said, "I tried to sleep tonight, but I couldn't. Every time I closed my eyes, you were there. But then when I opened them, you weren't. After a while, I couldn't take it anymore. So I walked to the kitchen and poured myself some—"

"Whiskey."

Ted laughed in surprise. "Do you have paparazzi spying on me?"

"I wouldn't give anyone that job but myself."

"Good to know." The ice tinkled again, then it sounded like he set down the glass.

"Haven't you ever wanted to see the Wyoming stars? Up close and personal?"

Eve counted her breaths, thinking she knew where he was going with this. *Hoping*. "I've heard they're spectacular."

"Much better view than in New York or Boston."

"I'd like to see them. Sometime."

"How about we make that time now?"

Eve's pulse thundered. She couldn't think of anything more romantic than an impetuous last-minute trip to Ted's ranch. "How will I get there?"

"I'll come and get you."

"When can you be here?"

"Fifteen minutes, tops."

Eve scrambled into her clothes, then raced to the bathroom to put on a dab of makeup. While she aimed to look natural, failing to conceal those under-eye circles wouldn't do. Plus, her cheeks needed a hint of color, as did her lips. She combed through her hair with her fingers and studied her reflection. *Much better.* She couldn't believe she was doing this. Running off to meet Ted in the middle of the night. That seemed so recklessly romantic. Eve had never had much excitement in her love life. Apart from that brief fling with Gustavo, she'd never really had much of a love life at all. All the men she'd dated had been like cookie-cutter replicas of each other. Young, upwardly mobile professionals with flat-screen TVs and incredible sound systems. They'd dressed alike and talked alike and seemed perfectly happy never to get out of Manhattan. Where was their sense of adventure? Their need to do something different? Break out of their shell? Even Gustavo in Spain seemed to have stuck to the life he'd been born with. Only Ted was different. And Eve found that difference exhilarating.

Ten minutes later, he met her in the lobby, which was empty at this hour apart from the lone bellhop manning the desk. Ted strode to her and swept her into his arms. "God, I missed you." Then, without seeming to care whether the bellhop was watching or not, he planted a scorchingly sexy kiss on her. His mouth was hot and hungry, setting her lips ablaze. Eve's knees buckled, but he steadied his embrace to hold her. He gazed down in her eyes and spoke in a sultry whisper. "Let's get out of here." Eve let him take her hand and lead her out the door, her whole world spinning. She'd never tasted passion like Ted's. Had never even known a man could possess it. And the wonderful thing was, all of Ted's passions were wrapped up in her.

"I'm glad you said yes," he told her once they were buckled in his SUV. Eve didn't know how she could have said no. It was becoming increasingly impossible to resist this man.

She answered with a flirtatious lilt, "You issue a pretty good invitation."

He reached out and took her hand. "This is crazy," he said, shaking his head. "Crazy, and I don't know what to do about it."

"Seems like you're already doing something."

He lifted her hand and gave the back of it a kiss. "Yeah." His grin broadened in the shadows. "You look beautiful tonight, you know that?"

Ted always made her feel pretty. It was in the way he looked at her. Every single time. A black cowboy hat sat on the console between them.

"Guess you won't be needing that on this trip," she said, deflecting the compliment.

"Sure I will." He gave her hand a squeeze, then set his grip on the wheel. "When the sun comes up, it can get pretty bright." He glanced at her in a playful way. "Hope you brought those shades."

"We're staying out all night?" she asked with surprise.

"After seeing the stars, I thought you might like to see a Wyoming sunrise. You play your cards right," he said with a wink, "you might even get me to fix you a Western omelet."

"Don't you have an adventure to lead in the morning?"

"Why don't we worry about tomorrow when the time comes. Meanwhile..." He stroked her cheek, and Eve's heart stilled. "Let's just focus on tonight."

They took the gravel drive to the back of the ranch way past the barn and the operational center for Wild West Brides. A rustic one-story house with tall windows snuggled up to the mountains. A small pond sat beside it ringed with pines, its waters glistening in the moonlight. "We'll see the stars better out back," he told her, parking the SUV in a spot by the house. It had a broad, covered front porch with a couple of rockers. You couldn't even see the other outbuildings from here. The location was totally private. Eve flushed, recalling how Ted liked to keep things that way.

"It's gorgeous out here," she said, catching her breath at the sight.

Ted scooted around the vehicle to open her door for her. "It's even better on the deck." He carried his cowboy hat in one hand and held her hand with his other.

"Thanks for coming out with me." His eyes shone in the darkness. He leaned forward and gave her a kiss. "I really missed you so badly. I know that it sounds—"

She brought a finger to his lips. "I missed you too."

He led her into the house, which was expansive and designed in a Western motif, with enormous antlers mounted over the huge stone hearth.

"Deer?" she asked him.

"Elk," he answered. "Same as the ones forming the arches in the town square. No worries, it's all eco-friendly.

Nobody hunted these animals down. They naturally shed these and leave them behind."

"Great to see you recycle."

Ted's laugh was warm and rumbly. "Papers, cans, and plastics too."

"You're some kind of modern cowboy."

He brought his arms around her and kissed her again. "And you're some kind of cub reporter." He whispered the words against her lips. "Just when are you going to write that story?"

Her breath was feathery and her head felt light. "Soon. But not tonight."

"Good."

He kissed her deeply then, and Eve felt she was falling away, into someplace deep and spiraling. A land she'd never visited before. "Want to see those stars?" he asked, pulling back.

Eve nodded, and he led her through the great room to a set of double-doors facing the mountains. He unlatched them and swung them open, letting in the cool night breeze. Eve stepped onto the deck and looked up, overwhelmed by the beauty. The sky was studded with stars that twinkled like diamonds in a velvet cape. Occasional wisps of clouds streaked behind them, crowning them with halos of white. "Oh my."

Ted drew close behind her, settling his arms around her waist.

He rasped against her neck, his breath tickling. "So, what do you think?"

Tingles tore down Eve's spine, sending current charging through her body.

"I've never seen anything like it."

Ted lightly pulled back her hair and brought his warm lips to her neck. "And I've never met anyone like you." He kissed her neck again, nibbling slightly. Eve gasped, her nipples hardening. "Ted."

"I've thought about you all night." He trailed kisses from her neck to the back of her ear. Eve's pulse fluttered. "I tried taking a shower…"

"A cold one?" she asked in a whisper.

Ted held her firmly to him, pressing his body close so she could sense his need. It was rock hard against her, centered in the small of her back. "I'll let you in on a secret," he growled in her ear. "It didn't work." Ted lowered his grip from her waist to her thighs, stroking them through the denim of her jeans. Eve's breasts and belly caught fire as she moaned back against him. "I need you, Eve," he said as his hands slid north. "Need you to be all mine." His palms traveled to her breasts, cupping them, caressing them, while he nibbled at the side of her neck, then her nape… then gave a playful nip at her shoulder.

Eve whimpered with desire. "Oh, Ted…"

His fingers began unbuttoning her blouse as the wind picked up in the valley. But Eve wasn't cold. She was steaming. Hot. Way hot. Hotter than boiling. Ted's hands slid under her bra, molding her flesh with his fingers, teasing her erect nipples. Eve felt moisture build below, as she throbbed between her legs. "I can't… take this."

"I'll stop if you want me to." Even as he said it, his hands slid smoothly down her rib cage, dipping into the waistband of her jeans. She would die if he stopped now.

"Don't you dare," she breathed, barely able to stand.

He groaned against her neck, pressing his erection more fully into her back as he undid and zipped down her jeans. "I want you." One hand tugged her jeans apart while the other glided over her panties. "Want you like I've never wanted any other woman."

Eve threw her head back with a cry as his fingers strummed lower, then lower still.

"Oh!" She gasped with delight, arching her back.

Wild winds blew, raking her hair, and fluttering her open blouse...lapping across her belly as her flesh moistened more and more. "You're so beautiful." The words were heated, heavy. "Just perfect." He dipped his hand into her panties, stroking her with tender skill. Eve cried out as his fingers found her, gently parting her folds. She was crazy with desire, desperate for his touch. Then he slowly slipped one finger inside. Eve gasped, her world gone hazy, bright sparkles shimmering around her. He moved into her with a gentle rhythm, and Eve felt that she might burst. Come apart at any minute. One hand cupped her breast while the other worked its magic between her legs. Eve threw her head back and moaned, not sure she could stand it another minute. "I want to take you back to the bedroom," he rasped against her cheek.

Eve nodded, gasping for air, not trusting her legs to support her. But she needn't have worried. Before she knew it, Ted had lifted her in his arms and was carrying her through the house. His dark eyes were sultry, demanding. "I'm going to love the daylights out of you," he said in a husky growl. "I hope you're ready."

Eve was more ready than she'd ever been. He'd driven her crazy on the deck. And that was just the appetizer. She was hungry for the main course. He laid her down on the bed, and Eve quickly rid herself of her clothing. Ted stepped out of his, pulling a foil packet from his pocket. "Are you...always...packing?" She meant to say it lightly, but passion threaded her voice, heating every breath.

"Only with you." He dropped his jeans to his knees and then his boxers too. Eve marveled at his size, recalling the feel of him. Needing to have him fill her again. He took out a sheath and slowly rolled it on. Her insides throbbed with anticipation.

Ted shucked the rest of his clothing and joined her on the bed. She looked up at him through the shadows filtering in through the still-open doors in the great room. Light gusts of air tickled their naked flesh.

Her words came out in an urgent rush. "Make love to me."

Ted shot her a sexy grin and gently parted her knees. "My pleasure."

He lowered himself to her, and Eve heard herself panting, sucking in rapid breaths just as she longed to draw Ted in. The tip of his erection found her, and her hips rose to meet him. She cried out, unable to stand it a second longer. "Please...now."

He entered her fully, and Eve gasped with delight when he filled her completely, then rocked forward. Eve gripped his strong shoulders, holding him tight as he rode her harder and harder. He groaned and gave her more, bucking toward her like a bronco, moaning for her again and again. Eve's back arched, her pleasure well rising, threatening to spill over. "Oh, Ted!"

His kisses were hot and hungry on her mouth and then her neck as he teased her breasts with one hand and supported himself on another. His tone was gravelly, out of control. "You could be"—he said, rocking into her—"the best thing...that's ever... Oh! Oh, Eve!" He arched suddenly, his stream erupting, and Eve arched with a cry to greet him, her peak matching his.

"I'm sorry," he whispered, collapsing on top of her and holding her close. "That was too soon."

"No," she said, kissing his lips. "It was just right."

Eve awoke five hours later to the sun streaming through the window. It opened on a gorgeous view showcasing a large grassy field and snowcapped mountains. "Coffee?" Ted asked, striding into the room. He wore a big, happy grin and his cowboy hat.

Eve sat up, still a bit groggy. Groggy but well satisfied. She certainly remembered that part. "You've been out already?"

He passed her the steaming mug, and she took a grateful sip. "Had to look in on the horses."

Ted sat down on the side of the bed and patted her hand. "I'm awfully glad you stayed over. We'll have to do it again sometime."

Eve giggled behind the rim of her mug, thinking she'd like nothing better. "Yes."

"In the meantime, I've made breakfast. I figured we could eat on the deck."

"That sounds amazing. But what about rafting?"

"We're meeting the group in your hotel lobby at nine. That gives us plenty of time to get you back early so you can freshen up."

Eve took another sip of coffee and cocked an eyebrow. "Got a shower here?"

He angled toward her. "Yeah."

"Maybe we can get in it together?"

Ted eyed her in a predatory way, then started to unbutton his shirt. He took her mug and set it aside. "Breakfast can wait."

He set his hat on the bed, and Eve tugged him toward her, kissing him firmly while running her hands across his muscled chest. All at once, she was hungry to have his power sweep over her again. To feel consumed by his passion. She wanted his body pressed to hers and needed to feel him inside her. The shower could wait.

Ted's eyebrows rose as her fingers found his belt and unhitched it. "I thought you wanted to shower."

"We'll do that next," she purred, pushing him down on the bed.

When Eve got back to her hotel, she had to hurry to get ready for her day. But all the rushing about was clearly worth it. She'd never had such a memorable night—or morning. They'd had to reheat the breakfast Ted had fixed in the microwave, but it still tasted delicious just the same. They hadn't had much time to linger over a second cup of coffee. Yet that was okay. Eve wouldn't change the way her time had gone with Ted for the world. Everything about her journey here had taken her by surprise. She'd certainly never expected to develop feelings for someone. Authentic feelings, and not just ones based on the role she'd come to play as a Wild West bride.

Ted had completely swept Eve off her feet. There was no denying it. And unless he'd read that silly acting book Glenn had tried to give her, Ted wasn't pretending either. He was falling for Eve too. Falling in some inexplicable way. Naturally, he had to get through this week and fulfill his role as the program's director. Just as Eve needed to finally buckle down and write her story. But once both those obligations were met, where would that leave things between Ted and Eve?

Her heart smarted at the possibility he might suggest this week be the end of it. That they stop things here and not ever try to see each other again. Yet the things he'd said and the way he'd been when he'd made love to her told Eve's heart a different story. She knew she and Ted would need to talk it over eventually and decide what their time here together meant for the two of them moving forward. But she didn't want to risk ruining things yet.

They still had today, then one final day of adventures, to get through. After that, there was Saturday, the wrapping-up day when all couples were supposed to go out for a parting lunch and discuss what came next before boarding their good-bye flights. If the topic happened to come up beforehand, Eve would be happy to discuss it with Ted. But she didn't want to be the one to broach the subject. Not now, not when everything was going so right. Besides, if Ted's answer wasn't the one she hoped for, she wasn't certain she was prepared to handle it. She'd never get her story done, and write it well, after that. Eve stopped herself as her neck flashed hot. She twisted up her hair and pinned it in place, thinking she didn't need to get ahead of herself. It was best to take things one step at a time. After all, one step at a time had worked so far.

Chapter Sixteen

By the time the raft returned to the dock, Eve's stomach was roiling. She'd met the group in the lobby at nine as planned, and she and Ted had played it cool, as if they still weren't officially together. And that was okay. She understood Ted's need to maintain a professional distance, and she appreciated keeping her love life private as well. Nobody had to know they were a couple for her to enjoy Ted's company. She'd been looking forward to a lovely morning with the perfect guy, before she realized rafts made her feel like vomiting.

Ted patted the back of her life vest. "You okay?"

Eve gripped the side of the raft and nodded. But inwardly she felt on the brink of passing out. It was a gorgeous day, and she should have enjoyed the adventure. Instead, she'd found the tumultuous ride over river rapids nauseating. The others had seemed to take it in stride, hooting and hollering as they'd risen—and fallen—over the crest of every wave. Eve's stomach lurched again, and she cupped her hand to her mouth.

"You look like you need to sit down," Ted whispered.

"I am sitting."

"I mean on dry land."

"My stomach's a little uneasy," she admitted quietly.

"Well, didn't we guess it!" a woman's voice proclaimed.

Eve looked up to find Ted's mom standing right in front of her. She and her husband were first in line to board the raft, after the current guests aboard exited. Bart's face beamed as he stood beside his wife. "It's all right," he offered in a hoarse whisper. "We know your secret."

"Secret?"

"Mom! Dad? What are you—"

"We signed up for the adventure," Lila said.

"She means the Adventure Package," Bart corrected. "We bought it at the hotel."

"Allows for horseback riding too." Lila adjusted her sunglasses. "Not that I'd suggest that for you, dear," she said, addressing Eve. "You probably shouldn't have been doing this either."

Eve glanced sideways at Ted, whose mouth hung open.

"Excuse me," a boatman said, urging them to step aside since they were blocking the egress of the others.

Ted stepped off first to offer Eve a steadying hand. "We're not sure what you're talking about," he told his parents when he was right beside them. "But I was meaning to talk to you later."

"One would hope so," Lila said with a little huff.

"Not that we blame *you*," Bart told Eve, a little louder than he should have. "Nobody's fault but his own that our boy can't keep his snake in his pants."

A hush fell over the crowd, and Eve's cheeks flamed. Ted, who still gripped her hand, squeezed it. "That was highly inappropriate," he told his dad with a combative glare. He slipped out of his life vest, then helped Eve with hers. "I suggest you apologize. To me, but especially to Eve."

"All aboard!" the captain called, breaking the awkward spell that had trapped Ted and his parents in an observation bubble. The gawkers finally ignored them and began hustling onto the raft. Eve spied Brian leading their group to the SUV in the distance and judged he was doing his friend a favor by getting them out of earshot.

Bart ignored his son and stared at his wife. Even she looked a bit embarrassed by Bart's outburst. "Line's moving, Lila."

"But Bart," she sputtered. "He was starting to say something about—"

"Doesn't matter, Mom." He gave each of his parents a hard stare. "I've changed my mind."

Then Ted tugged Eve away, toward the parking area. Once they were clear of the dock, Ted tried to release her hand, but she held on firmly. "I'm sorry, Ted," she said with sympathy.

He stopped walking and met her eyes. "I'm sorry you were exposed to that."

"It wasn't your fault."

"Can't help who you're born to."

"Maybe you're adopted?"

Ted burst out laughing. "If that was meant to lighten my mood, it worked." He leaned forward and lightly pecked her on the lips.

"But Brian! And the others?"

"Truthfully, Eve? I no longer care." He studied her with warm brown eyes. "Do you?"

"About what they think?" she asked sweetly. "Not really."

"We didn't mean for this to happen."

"No."

"But something has."

"Yes."

"And I don't want it to stop."

She tilted her chin up to gaze at him. "Me either."

"Then it won't." He pulled her to him and kissed her lightly on the forehead. "I'm glad you didn't let my parents ruin it for you. For me. For both of us."

She hugged him back. "You're your own man."

He pulled back to gaze in her eyes. "You don't know how happy it makes me to hear you say that."

Lila admonished Bart as they each clung to their paddles. The raft was rocketing over waves, and both hung on for dear life. "I think you were a little hard on him, Bart."

"Me? You're the one who said the girl was too preggers for pony riding!"

"Well, she probably is!"

"This is just like Ted." Bart clucked his tongue. "Knocking one girl up wasn't enough. He had to go for two."

"It's not fair to bring up Rebecca." She waited until they'd crested another wave. "Besides, Ted said that wasn't true. That she'd made the whole thing up."

"Poppycock. You think I believe that for a second?" Bart turned to look at her. "He took care of it, that's what he did. One way or another."

She flipped her shades up on her head to stare at him. "I don't believe you. Don't believe that for a minute. That's not my son you're talking about. Theodore lives up to his responsibilities."

"Sure he does. Just like staying in law school."

Lila frowned.

"The fact is, Lila, you don't even *know* who we're talking about. Neither do I. The boy's been lying to us all along. Who really knows where the falsehoods stop and the truth begins?"

She flipped her shades back down and turned away, not daring to look at her husband. Because, the sad fact was, he had a point.

Later that afternoon, Ted sat across from Eve in a cozy café. The place was mainly a confectionary shop known for its exquisite chocolates, but he'd assured her the coffee was dynamite too. She took a sip from her steaming cappuccino, obviously appreciating his decision.

"Delicious coffee. Great rec."

"Plus," he said, leaning toward her, "it's quiet. Off the beaten path."

"You seem to favor faraway spots." She shot him a saucy look, and Ted's pulse pounded. "Places that are nice and private."

For an instant, he had the crazy notion to forget all about business and haul Eve back to her hotel room. "You keep tempting me that way, we might never get through this interview."

She grinned, but her cheeks were flushed.

"Mind if I record this?" she asked, indicating a device.

Ted pulled a pen from his pocket. "Thanks for reminding me. I almost forgot to give this back."

"Ah," she said, eyeing the logo. "Yes. I've certainly missed it." She set it beside a small notepad, then switched on her recorder.

"Your hair looks great down."

She flipped the recorder off.

"And up." He gave her a sultry perusal. "I like it both ways." He lowered his voice to a whisper and caught some of her curls in his hand. "But mostly I like running my fingers through it."

"Will you stop already?" But inside, her heart was light. It felt so good to be with Ted and banter this way. No matter what they did, they seemed to get along so well.

He pasted on a dour expression. "If I must."

Eve giggled and turned her recorder back on, shooting him a warning glance.

"*So*... Tell me about how you first thought up Wild West Brides."

"Some of it's personal."

"Too personal to print?"

"I'll promise to tell you the truth if you'll airbrush certain parts."

"I'll leave out anything you want me to."

He downed the small espresso that he'd taken black, then paused a beat, gathering his thoughts. "It all started with Rebecca."

Eve blinked, seeming surprised that he'd go there. "Your old girlfriend from law school?"

"That's the one."

"What about her?"

Ted rested his elbows on the table. "You know that thing they say about learning things from other people? Both good and bad?"

Eve nodded.

"Well, Rebecca was the person who taught me all about what a relationship shouldn't be."

"Oh."

"I don't mean to sound negative. But she did me pretty wrong. It took a long time to get over it."

"But you are...?" She hesitated. "Over it?"

"Yes." He gave her a deep, meaningful look. "One hundred percent certain."

The tiny worry lines creasing her eyes eased. "I'm glad."

He reached out and took her hand. "Me too."

"I guess what's safe to print is that I learned from experience that not every couple in this world is meant to be together. Then there are others that seem… I don't know…" He glanced at her. "Fated."

"You thought you could help fate along with your algorithms?"

"Exactly. Although the computer program was really Brian's brainchild. He's always been a computer wiz, and when I started talking to him about the idea, he said he could find a way to work with it."

"You met Brian in law school?"

"No. Playing pickup soccer. There was this local intramural club I was a part of. Brian wasn't in it, but one of his friends asked him to come along. We seemed to work well together on the field, and after a while wound up together on other sports teams. After playing, we'd sometimes grab a beer, discuss our women problems and life's challenges."

Eve was clearly intrigued by his story. "Was Brian seeing Mary then?"

"Nope." His lips parted in a grin. "He found her using his algorithms."

"Did not!"

"It's the God's honest truth. Brian offered to serve as a guinea pig for his new invention. We recruited a small test group from the local area by placing a 'Fast Date' ad on line."

"Fast Date? What's that?"

"It was sort of like a speed-dating thing. We brought five men and five women together to discuss a preselected topic and guaranteed that each person would find at least one match they could talk to."

"How could you make that promise?"

"Brian had them all fill out his questionnaire first. He had all the matches pegged in advance but wanted to give each couple the chance to find each other on their own."

"Fascinating. What did the couples discuss?"

"The prompt was *what's the most adventuresome thing you'd like to do?*"

"Was that asked in Brian's questionnaire?"

"No. It was just a fun way to get people talking. And, boy, did it ever! We set the whole thing up in a local pub where Brian and I knew the bartender. Couples sat at tables and only had five minutes each to swap answers to that question. We asked them to write their most memorable answers down for our records. And those answers surprised us."

"Why?"

"Most had to do with things set out west. Or things one could do out west. Like horseback riding, whitewater rafting…"

"Paragliding?"

"Yep."

"The seeds of Wild West Brides*.*"

"The energy in the room was phenomenal, Eve. And when the right couples came together—I mean the ones Brian had predicted would be a match—you could practically see sparks flying."

"You didn't want to participate?"

"Somebody had to run the show. Besides, Brian was already in it. Way deep."

"Something like a scientist testing his own potion?" Eve asked with a laugh.

Ted chuckled in return. "Precisely." He drew a breath and released it. "Anyway! That's where it all started, at Musket Joe's. That was the name of the bar," he explained to her inquiring look. "Afterward, Brian and I did follow up with the couples to see how everything had gone. Of course, Brian didn't have to check up on one of the pairings." He shot Eve a wink. "He already had evidence that one had worked out."

"Mary came with him to Wyoming?"

"They're getting married next month."

"Oh, how sweet! I hadn't a clue." She sipped from her cup. "I'd love to meet her sometime."

He met her gaze and held it. "I'm sure you will."

Eve checked the time on her recorder. "How soon after that field test did you and Brian decide to make your move to Jackson Hole?"

"About two months. It didn't take much to see the idea of forming Wild West Brides was much more exciting to me than staying in law school. Besides, it gave me the chance to do the most adventuresome thing I'd ever wanted to do."

"What was that?"

He took both her hands in his with a warming grin.

"Be a cowboy."

Eve kissed Ted good-bye in the lobby, not daring to let him come upstairs to her room. She had a rough draft to get out and wanted to stay in and work on it while her conversation with Ted was fresh in her mind. She had notes on her recorder but didn't really need them. She recalled everything Ted had told her with vivid detail. Including the part about him being well over his ex. Eve's heart bounded at the thought this might mean he was seriously taken with her. While he'd hinted at that, more than once by now, it almost seemed too good to be true.

Ted appeared kind, considerate, and warm. Not only that, he was incredibly adventuresome too. Way more so than she was, although she found herself willing to learn. Eve was still unsure about paragliding tomorrow. That sounded like really pushing the envelope. Especially for someone like her. But if Ted was flying with her, as he'd promised her he would, maybe she'd be willing to try it. Somehow, by being with Ted, Eve felt there was nothing she couldn't do. Other than perhaps convince his parents to like her, and accept Ted's choices too. Eve frowned and clicked on her e-mail, sending her file attachment on its way.

She'd written a good story and had made Ted sound captivating besides. Not that this was much work. He was charismatic enough on his own. His personality leapt right off the page. It was too bad he was at odds with his parents. She hoped there was a way to fix that but wasn't sure. Being raised by a single dad, Eve had never had two parents of her own and felt it was a shame that Ted did but was estranged from them. She really hoped he would talk to them, and that they'd find a way to work things out. But at this point, she just didn't know. It was hard for her to guess what Ted might do.

Eve was just standing to stretch her legs when someone knocked at the door. She couldn't imagine who it might be at this hour. She checked the clock. It was just past eight thirty. Eve parted the door a crack and peered out at Ted, standing there as handsome as ever, holding a huge box of pizza and an open bottle of wine. "Room service?" He grinned, and his smile sent electric current traveling down her spine.

"Ted!"

"Did you get the story off?" he asked, lowering the box in his hand.

"Just now."

"Perfect." She stepped aside, and he walked into her room to set the pizza and wine on the table. "I thought we'd celebrate." He took her in his arms, and Eve sighed against him.

"It's pretty hard to refuse a big, strong cowboy. Especially one bearing pizza."

Ted laughed and gave her a kiss. "I thought you might need a break. I hadn't planned to stay…"

She snuggled in his embrace. "Well, now that my story's done…"

"Thought it was just a first draft?"

"It was."

"Going to need revisions?"

"Mm-hm."

He leaned forward and lightly nibbled her bottom lip. A breath escaped her. "Ted."

He removed his cowboy hat and tossed it onto the bed. "Yes, darling?"

"How about we have some wine?"

"I'm up for that."

He pulled her to him and kissed her again until she moaned. Ted was apparently up for other things too, and Eve was desperate for him to give them to her. She didn't know what it was about Ted, but she'd never felt so utterly attracted to a man. It was like she couldn't keep her hands off of him. Already, she was unbuttoning his shirt.

He helped her along, mumbling between warm, wet kisses, "The pizza will get cold."

Eve steered him toward the bed and purred into his mouth, "I love cold pizza."

"What a coincidence," he said with a growl. "So do I."

Two hours later, Eve woke up under the covers, snuggled in Ted's arms. She sighed happily, realizing this wasn't another crazy cowboy dream. She was really here with him.

"Awake?" he asked, nuzzling the back of her neck with his lips.

Little shivers tore down her spine, then sparked like electric current around her hips. All of a sudden, she was throbbing again. Needing him. "A little."

Ted rolled her onto her back with a laugh. "How'd you like to be a lot?" he asked with a predatory whisper.

"I think I'd like that," she whispered back. In the quiet of the room, there were almost no sounds between them, only his occasional groans of pleasure and her moans of satisfaction. Sheets rustled as he held her, and they whispered words Eve never thought she'd hear. Out of the blue and faraway in Wyoming, here she was, falling in love.

Chapter Seventeen

Later that night, she and Ted sat up in bed, eating ice cream. He'd ordered them a room-service sundae to share.

"This goes perfectly with the red wine," she said, taking another rich, creamy bite.

"Mmm." He leaned forward and licked her lips. "You're covered in chocolate."

She lifted an eyebrow. "Not as much as I could be."

"You better watch that," he said with a husky growl. "You could be asking for trouble."

A happy laugh escaped her. "I think I've had all the *trouble* I can stand for one evening. I'm starting to feel like I've been horse riding."

Ted bellowed a laugh. "I wouldn't want to overwork you."

"No. You either."

"Not a chance." He grinned and settled back against the headboard, tucking her under one arm. "I can't believe the fun I'm having. We're having." He glanced at her uncertainly. "I hope you are too."

"Oh, Ted," she said, massaging his rock-solid chest, "I'm having the very best time. Thank you."

He set aside the ice-cream bowl and kissed the top of her head. "Better than you thought you'd have in Wyoming?"

"Way better. Everything has surprised me. *You've* surprised me."

"I guess life has surprised us both," he said, holding her close.

Eve couldn't recall ever feeling happier than she did at this moment. If only there was a way to have it go on forever.

Eve's cell buzzed on the nightstand, and Ted checked the clock. "Who's texting you at midnight?"

He picked it up to pass to her.

"The only one I know who works this late is—"

"Glenn?" he asked, glancing down at the message that popped up on the screen.

Get out of town! Boston?

Ted's mouth took a downward turn, and Eve's heart jolted.

"Here, let me see that," she said.

He slowly passed it over.

Ted was eying her in an odd way, a way that made her insides feel all squishy. "Who's Glenn?" he asked flatly.

"He's um… Sort of like a friend. Yeah, that, but not romantic."

"I was worried it was somebody you worked with."

Eve's pulse pounded in her ears so loudly she couldn't hear herself think. "What?"

"I'd hate to think you'd do that, Eve. But I know now that you wouldn't. If he's just a friend and you shared something in confidence…" He jostled her in his arms with an uneasy laugh. "I mean, it's not like it's going to print."

He pulled her up against him and laid her head against his chest, his heart lightly thudding underneath. "I've just had my fair share of deception, you know?" His fingers strummed her hair. "That's what happened with Rebecca. It's taken me a long time to learn not everybody's like that. I'm sorry. Sorry that I'd even think you'd—"

Eve sat up to look at him, her voice trembling. "No, I'm the one who's sorry. That Glenn… He *is* a person I work with."

"What do you mean?"

"I didn't think it was wrong. I mean, you told me everything in the interview."

"About how Brian and I started Wild West Brides, yes."

"So I didn't think you'd mind the funny story about your parents, or how—"

"My *parents*?" His expression darkened. "You didn't."

"I didn't mention any incidents, just that you didn't have their approval to—"

"Unbelievable." Ted abruptly pushed back the covers and dropped his feet to the floor. "That's incredible to me you'd do that. My family information is personal."

"I know! I didn't put in any details. I airbrushed it like you told me."

He narrowed his eyes at her. "You mentioned Rebecca, didn't you?"

"Not by name. Only to say you were getting over a broken—"

"Jesus, Eve!" His voice boomed as he leapt from the bed. "Is nothing sacred to you? I told you that in confidence."

"You agreed to tell your story!"

"You promised to leave my personal life out of it, which clearly included Rebecca. I told you what was fit to print at the coffee shop. That other stuff, everything I said in the park... That was just between us. You agreed!"

"That was before. It seemed that afterward, you were cool with..."

He stepped into his boxers, then nabbed his jeans from a nearby chair. "You were supposed to be writing an article, for crying out loud. Not a freaking exposé."

"I don't think I did anything wrong," she said, flustered. All of a sudden, everything seemed to have taken a wrong turn. She'd written a very flattering piece. And the things she'd put in were just backstory. "What I mean is—"

He met her gaze with a stormy look. But this time there was something other than ire in his eyes. His voice quaked. "I *trusted* you."

"For heaven's sake, Ted! You're from Boston!"

"And you're from Virginia!"

"Yes!"

"But you live in New York."

"I don't follow what you're saying."

"You didn't stay where you came from. You moved somewhere else to find your way, to work as a writer. But I'd never so much as *presume* to call you a fake."

"But I didn't—"

"Oh yes, you did." He slid on his jeans, then stepped into his boots and buttoned his chambray shirt. "You promised me, Eve. *Promised* not to blow my cover. It's part of my shtick. The whole operation here."

"That was before, for the group!"

"What about the hundreds of groups in the future? Wild West Brides' future clients?"

"They'll still come! They'll come in droves!"

"That is not what I gave you permission to print."

"That is *not* your journalistic decision."

His lips drew a cold hard line. "I see."

"Ted, this is getting ridiculous."

"It certainly is." He set his hat on his head and tapped it in place.

"I can't believe that you're leaving. That you'd go. Just like that."

"I've spent my whole life trying to get people to respect who I am. But at base, I understand I've got to respect myself. *You're* the one who came out here pretending to be someone you weren't. This guy here? Is the same Ted Walker that said Howdy when you got on that horse. It doesn't matter where I come from, what I did before, or who my parents are. All that matters is who I am in here." He slapped his chest. "And that I'm leading the life I want."

She was stung by his words but even more so by his tone. And all that anger was directed at her. "I know," she said, her voice cracking. "I agree." She grabbed the coverlet to her chest and tried to slide toward him, but he stepped away.

"But you know the worst thing? The thing that really burns?" Fire brimmed in his eyes. "You *used me* for your story."

"*No.*"

"Tell me one thing, Eve. When you came out to Wyoming, was bedding a 'real cowboy' part of the plan?"

"No! I swear! I never…"

"Well, I guess I've been a disappointment on all counts."

Eve steadied her bottom lip and fought back her tears. She drew a breath. "I never thought this would happen. It's all been a terrible mistake."

She'd said that referring to their misunderstanding, but he clearly took her to mean getting involved with him had been the giant misstep. "You're damn straight, it has."

He met her gaze, but his eyes were cold. "Well, you got what you came for, didn't you?"

"I got my article, yes."

"Then there's nothing more holding you back."

Maybe there isn't. For a crazy, lunatic moment, she'd thought she and Ted were developing something. Something magical. Something potentially serious. She'd never been more wrong. If he could judge her like this, without even giving her a chance… He hadn't even *read* her piece, and already she was tried and convicted. She'd thought the background stuff made it more interesting. Appealing to readers. Ted's was a fascinating story that deserved to be shared. Eve's head spun. Up until now, she'd thought he'd been on board with it. How could she have been so wrong?

He strode toward the door with a purposeful air and cracked it open. Before he left, he spoke without looking over his shoulder. "The group leaves for paragliding at ten. If you're not in the lobby, nobody will miss you." Then he opened the door and shut it behind him with a *bang*.

Eve cupped her hand to her mouth. Tears streamed down her face, running hard and fast, burning trails down her cheeks and splattering onto the coverlet still clenched in her hands. "Oh my God, oh my God…" she heaved. Her stomach churned and her chest ached, threatening to burst open. What had she been thinking coming here? And how had she let herself become involved with Ted? Opening herself up to *this*? Pain seared through her, and she doubled forward in sobs again. She was right when she told him it had been a mistake, because it had been. *All of it.*

Chapter Eighteen

Ted rode the ski lift car to the top of the mountain at Teton Village with the others. You had to be a certified instructor to carry a glider with you, so every one in their party had been assigned a pilot Ted knew. Brian leaned toward him as they approached their destination at the run's highest peak. "Eve didn't feel like flying?"

"Might already be on her plane." He tried unsuccessfully to conceal the bitter edge to his voice. While Ted felt bad about the words they'd had last night, the truth was Eve had done very little to defend herself. And there was almost no defending what she'd done.

She'd practically accused him in print of being a counterfeit cowboy. Of not really being who he was. Not only that, she'd broken his confidence. And that had stung plenty. Well, who needed her anyway? He certainly didn't. Just because she looked good and kissed well and had pretended to really care. Ha! Who was the big, fat fake now?

"You okay, buddy?" Brian asked

Ted shifted the gear in his hands. "Yeah, I'll be fine." But in his heart, he sure didn't feel like it.

Later that afternoon, Ted met his parents at their upscale hotel bar for high tea and crumpets. His mom's idea. It didn't escape Ted that his dad was drinking bourbon.

"You want something?" Bart asked when Ted joined them at their elegant table with a view of Grand Teton beyond the golf course.

"I'll just stick with water. I'm not staying."

"We wish you would," Lila pleaded. "We want to apologize." She glanced at her husband. "Don't we, Bart?"

Bart swigged from his bourbon and grunted. "I don't see how you couldn't tell us about the baby," he said gruffly.

"Baby?" Ted asked with surprise.

"We can see a misdirection of career," his mom went on. "The fact that you're still trying to find yourself. But your father's right, son. As the grandparents-to-be, we had a right to know."

His dad set down his glass. "You didn't even tell us about the last one."

"The last one was a hoax!"

A server appeared with a teapot and turned over the cup that had been positioned upside-down on a saucer. Ted was too distracted by his parents to decline the tea. "I'd appreciate it very much if someone could fill me in on what's going on," he said once their server had poured for him and his mom and left.

"Your Eve…" His mom lowered her voice. "We understand she's pregnant."

Ted stared at them both in shock. "By whom?"

His folks exchanged stunned glances. "You mean," his mom asked gingerly, "you didn't know?"

"I can't even imagine what would make you think that."

"She was sick on the raft," Bart said.

"Plus, you're planning to marry."

"Marry?" Ted took a swallow of tea, grateful for something to clear his throat. Of all the women in the world he might choose as a lifetime partner, it certainly wouldn't be some conniving, disloyal redhead from New York! Virginia. Wherever.

"Isn't that why you're going through with it?" his mom asked in a whisper.

"Because she has a bun in the oven?" Bart quietly piped in.

"I wouldn't marry Eve Parker if she were the last woman on earth," Ted asserted coldly.

"Then why were you two all over each other?" his mom asked.

"Certainly looked serious to me," Bart agreed.

Ted studied them, then massaged his brow. What was this? Had his parents been spying on them? Where? How many times? "Look, Eve is a long story. But the truth is, it's none of your business."

"It should be," Bart said.

"Why?"

Lila's expression softened. "Because we care about you. Whether or not you believe it, it's true." Ted surveyed his mom's face in the afternoon shadows, admitting to himself that for the first time, she looked motherly. Like she was actually capable of tender emotion. Not that she'd ever shown him much before.

Bart hung his head and grumbled into his bourbon before flagging the server over for another shot. "I'm sorry I embarrassed you down by the river."

"We both are," Lila said. "And that we were rude to your girl."

His dad met his gaze. "That's not the way we meant to get started."

"He means with our new daughter-in-law," Lila added. Then she continued sadly, "We're sorry if our behavior caused some sort of spat between you."

"And it apparently has," Bart confirmed.

Ted started to protest, but his dad stopped him. "Where is she? We'd like to tell her ourselves. Maybe if we apologize, you and she can make up."

"Yes," Lila said brightly. "We'd like to ask her to dinner. Get to know her."

Ted ran a hand through his hair. "I'm afraid that won't be possible."

"Why not?" his folks asked together.

Ted looked from one to the other. "She's left town."

"Oh!" His mom's face registered surprise.

"Was this on account of...?" his dad began.

"It had nothing to do with either of you," Ted said, even though that wasn't entirely true. "It was strictly between Eve and me. But now, it's over."

"You're not planning to get married?" Lila asked.

"Mom, that was never on the table."

For the life of him, his mom looked genuinely disappointed. Unbelievably, so did his dad. She patted Bart's arm, and his eyes held agreement. "We're so sorry, son."

"This whole trip has been a disaster," Bart grumbled.

"Your dad's tournament was canceled," Lila explained.

Of course, Ted thought. *Golf.*

"And then there was that unsettling business about law school," his mom continued.

Ted started to stand, but Bart reached out a hand to stop him. "Where are you going?"

"To find more accepting company."

"Sit down and stop being so stubborn," the older man groused. "You can't blame us for being in shock. As far as we knew, you were still in California."

"You could have told us," Lila said softly.

"No. I don't believe I could have."

"Why not?" Bart wanted to know. "Are you ashamed of what you do?"

"Ashamed?" Ted felt himself flush. "Not at all! I run a great business. I'm proud of it."

"What is it you do exactly?" Lila asked.

Ted glanced at them in surprise. "Honestly?"

Bart met his son's eyes. "We both want to know."

"So you can tell me I'm wrong?"

"I thought you said business was good?" Bart quipped.

"It is. We're thinking of developing a franchise."

"Ted," his mom said, pleased. "That's fantastic!"

"What's the name of this business?" Bart asked. "The one that you've started?"

Ted hesitated a moment, avoiding his dad's eyes. "Wild West Brides."

"What?" Bart sputtered.

But Lila just gave him a genuine grin. "I think that's darling!"

A few nights later, Ted sat on his deck drinking whiskey—straight up. It was hard not to think about Eve and the time they'd shared here. Now Ted was sorry he'd ever brought her to his house. Her memory haunted the place: the fine scent of her perfume still lingering in the sheets in the bedroom. Ted took another swig of liquor, but its heat in his mouth only reminded him of her. How could he have been so naïve? He'd trusted Eve way too quickly and with too much information. Now look what she'd gone and done with it! Or what she was about to do. The new month's issue of her magazine hadn't hit the stands yet. He'd searched for it with worry online, thinking that maybe an electronic version would get released earlier. Ted was awfully bitter that Eve would drag his folks into it and really hoped her mention of them wasn't unflattering. She had no business sticking her nose into that anyway. Ted had planned to deal with them in his own time, and he already had. They'd surprised him with their interest in his business. His dad had even shocked him by saying those five little words Ted never thought he'd hear him say. *"I'm proud of you, son."*

Ted took another belt and set down his glass, gazing up at the stars. They were still as bright as ever, but deep down in his soul, it sure felt like rain. His parents had left Jackson Hole this morning, along with the rest of the group from Wild West Brides. As he and Brian had predicted, the two happy couples made plans to see each other again. And Danni was taking Chet home to meet her family. Ted tried not to think about what it might be like taking Eve to Boston. There was so much he could show her there... *If she weren't the callous player who'd just trounced my heart,* Ted reminded himself.

He didn't know how he could have been so wrong about her, but he guessed he had been. Wonderful. Now he'd had two women deceive him by pretending to be something they weren't. That was probably what made the situation with Eve sting so badly. *Fool me once, shame on you. Fool me twice...* Ted knew he should have seen it coming, but he'd somehow been blindsided by the whole thing. It was hard to believe Eve had faked it. But that was certainly how it seemed. She'd not just falsified her information on the Wild West Brides application form, she'd duped Ted into believing her feelings for him were authentic. They'd certainly felt that way when she'd been in his arms.

Ted sadly shook his head, determined to pack these thoughts away. He had a new Wild West Brides group arriving tomorrow and needed to play his cowboy role for as long as it lasted. Who knew how long that would be once Eve's story went to press? The damndest thing was, Ted didn't feel like a fake one bit. When he'd told Eve that what mattered was what was on the inside, he'd meant every word. Ted stared up at the big Wyoming sky, knowing it would always believe him. The ranch and his horse Tex would be there for him too. He didn't need some woman in New York to verify who he was. All Ted had to do was listen to his heart.

Chapter Nineteen

Four weeks later, Eve pulled the pen from her hair and thumped it against her desk. She was supposed to meet with Ross at eleven, but he'd been called into some last-minute meeting upstairs. Glenn strolled over and obtrusively opened her bottom desk drawer. "What? No Milky Milanos?"

"I've given them up," Eve said. "Along with the other dangerous things in my life."

"Like matadors and cowboys?" Glenn leaned a hip against her desk, but she ignored him. Not that she'd told Glenn anything about her personal relationship with Ted. He'd come to the conclusion all on his own that something more than sheer journalism had taken place out west. And he still couldn't get that blasted Spain story straight. Never had.

Finally, her desk phone rang, and she picked it up. It was Ross. He wanted her in his office in five minutes.

"I hope it's good news."

Eve held up a hand. "Fingers crossed."

"You don't need luck to help you," Glenn said kindly. "I read your polish, and you killed it. That's a great article you did. Even if it *was* a month late."

"Thanks."

"What I don't get is… Who was the girl who got away? The one bride in the group who didn't work out?"

"Names were changed to protect the innocent."

"Right."

Five minutes later, Ross handed her an envelope with a smile.

"What's this?"

"Your bonus!"

"Bonus? I didn't know anything about—"

"No, but it was spectacular, Eve. And *so* worth the wait! *So much emotion...* It was almost like you were writing about yourself."

"Ha-ha."

Ross eyed her a moment. "You weren't, were you?"

"Of course not!" she protested just a little too quickly.

"Well, anyhow, even if you were, I can hardly see how that matters. The fact is you nailed it. Put together a genuine human-interest piece exposing a glowing business practice, as well as the chinks in the armor."

"Chinks?"

"Nothing is foolproof, of course. Your piece proves it. While Wild West Brides might work for some, it most certainly can't accommodate everybody. Despite what their glossy brochures promise."

Eve's heart sank. Was she doing the wrong thing in letting this go to print? It wasn't really fair to paint herself as a jilted bride when she'd never fully participated in the program. She hadn't even legitimately filled out the questionnaire. "You don't think this will hurt Ted's business?" she asked tentatively.

"Hurt it? Sweetheart, haven't you heard? *There's no such thing as bad publicity.*"

She weighed the envelope in her hand. "Maybe not, but I'd still hate to think that I was responsible for—"

Without warning, Ross snatched the envelope away. "Having second thoughts now, are we?"

"No!"

Ross fanned the envelope in the air. "Listen, Eve. Everything you said about Ted was flattering. The way he and Brian had field-tested their idea, how he'd put every bit of his personal savings into the outfit hoping to make it fly. I can't imagine any reader would hold him accountable for *one relationship* that didn't work out because the guy involved pretended to be something he wasn't. And—hoo boy, wasn't this rich?—the girl was pretending too! You said yourself that was against the Wild West Brides code of ethics."

"Yes, but—"

"Though, it didn't really seem like her fault, now did it? It was almost like *he* was the pot calling the kettle black and wouldn't even hear her out. She seemed like such a sweetheart too. Really genuine and heartbroken." Ross sighed. "It's a miracle you got that exclusive."

"Yeah, but the guy... If you read it, you saw that he was hurting also."

"I *know*. Really got to me." Ross clutched his chest. "Right here. It was almost like one of those reality shows."

"And the two of them got voted off the island?"

"More like neither one got the rose."

"Maybe it's a little too melancholy."

"No, no! This will get to our audience, I guarantee it. Whether the female populace will want to marry Ted or throttle him after learning what his business put that poor girl through, I can't say. But I *can* wager lots of ladies will be flocking to Wyoming. Just to see for themselves."

Eve swallowed hard. "See what?"

Ross smiled broadly. "Why, the man who started it all, of course. Handsome Westerner Ted Walker!" He flipped to the glossy photo attached to the file on his desk. "He *is* one dishy cowboy."

Eve stewed all the way back to her desk. This article wasn't having the intended outcome at all! When she'd rewritten it, she'd been bruised. And, okay, maybe had taken the fallout from her relationship with Ted a little more personally than she should have. But didn't that prove that Ted was no relationship expert? How could she write something promising millions of women they could find their happily ever afters in Jackson Hole when she knew from personal experience Ted's promises didn't always ring true?

Hadn't he intimated he was falling for her? She knew she hadn't imagined him telling her he didn't want whatever was developing between them to stop. He'd hinted at lots more besides that. She had it on audiotape! And then, with very little reason at all, he'd practically tossed her out of the state. Not a very endearing way to treat the woman charged with writing your publicity piece.

Still, she'd thought enough of him to rewrite her original draft. While she aimed to be a hardnosed reporter, she wasn't bent on destroying people's lives. Ted had a right to his privacy, and so did his parents and former girlfriend. So she'd removed the background references entirely. Instead, she'd written just what Ted had suggested. All about how he and Brian had conceived the program—and that he'd learned from previous experience what did and didn't make a relationship work. Ha! He'd learned well enough to know how to end one. *With a bang.*

Eve felt a burning ache inside, still smarting from his parting allegations. He'd accused her of taking advantage of him, and of using him just for a story. While that was the original reason she'd gone to Wyoming, that certainly hadn't been the end game once she'd gotten to know him. It was like he was ready to judge her in an instant without giving her half a chance. Well, fine. Maybe that wasn't a chance that she wanted anyway.

Eve sat heavily in her chair and popped open the seal on the envelope. She was stunned to see it contained more than just a check—a very large one. It also contained some kind of correspondence, neatly folded into thirds, business style. She opened it, then stared, holding the page with trembling fingers. It was an employment offer. She'd been promoted!

And not just to Winnie's job. She was being appointed to Jackie's. Associate editor in charge of reporting! It was an excellent post and one that involved flexibility. She could work from home, or nearly anywhere in the country, really. A lot could be done online. She'd only occasionally have to put in face time at the office. She'd travel a lot for interviews, but the magazine would foot the bill. It was a dream assignment in every way. She'd heard through the rumor mill that Jackie wasn't returning. That she'd decided to stay home with the baby and freelance. But until now, Eve hadn't believed it was true.

She knew she should feel ecstatic, but the truth was she wasn't. This bonus and new job felt like ill-gotten gains. She hadn't written the article she was supposed to, the clear-cut one about Ted and his business. She'd sullied it with her own sour grapes, daring to cast aspersions on the entire outfit just because her pitiful romance hadn't worked out. While her tale was honest and heartfelt, was it really fair to include it?

Eve's heart was at war with her head. In one way, she believed the new article to be strong. She'd also convinced herself it told the truth. It was ridiculous to believe that Brian's program was foolproof. But because she hadn't tried it herself, maybe it was wrong of her to condemn it. She was supposed to have been profiling a business and not picking apart its owner. Although her own battered heart had certainly been beaten up enough by him.

She thought she'd been taking the higher road by leaving out mention of Ted's former lover and his parents, and keeping his little secret about who he really was. But if her motives were so grand, why did she feel so totally terrible about them now? She knew precisely why. It was because she'd included that tiny bit of fiction at the end. That little vignette about how Wild West Brides worked great for most but certainly didn't suit all. She'd gone on to detail one little love story gone amiss. It was all about a trusting lovelorn woman and a guy who'd faked his identity. Never mind that the woman had fudged a few things in her own application as well.

Eve swallowed hard, the truth hitting her hard like a sucker punch. Even her fiction had been embellished too much. And was probably more than a little unfairly slanted in the woman's direction. Ted had been right in accusing Eve of joining in the group under false pretenses. In many ways, Eve had been far more deceitful than Ted ever had been. Right down to the final paragraph of her...exposé.

The back of Eve's neck felt hot, and she grabbed a pen off her desk to put up her hair. She stared at it in surprise, realizing it was the one Ted had given her. The one embossed with the logo from Wild West Brides.

"Fine!" Eve said out loud. "So the universe wants to send me a sign! I'm a dummy! A big, stinking dummy!" She was too, and she knew it. Eve had poured all her energy into crafting her article, but—after all this time— she still didn't have the story straight. *I'll never get it right unless I started playing by the rules. And those rules said you couldn't go calling yourself an authority on what did and didn't work without ever really testing it yourself.* This was why she'd had that unsettled feeling in her gut. It wasn't so much about the "couple that didn't work out" in her story as it was about her. She'd written about her and Ted, but that had been wrong. Neither of them had officially been a part of the program. Ted had never completed a profile, as far as Eve knew. The one thing she knew for certain was that she hadn't done one herself. Perhaps if she had, she would have been paired with someone suitable. Wild West Brides might even have found her the perfect match. Someone destined for her based on her legitimate information.

Fire crept up her chin and fanned across her cheeks as Eve realized what a big, fat phony she'd been. Well, maybe it was time to turn things around and start being the girl her encouraging dad always said she could be. *Play to your strengths, Eve.* Oh yeah? What were those? Eve was inquisitive. She wanted to know things. And, now more than ever, she needed to know the truth. Maybe Wild West Brides really was some sort of matchmaking godsend. Maybe Ted and Brian's program really *could* bring happy couples together by giving fate a hand. If she found that to be the case, wouldn't she need to report it rather than downplaying the group's success rate by including an unwarranted account of her own? Eve badly wanted Jackie's job, but she didn't want it badly enough to sacrifice who she was in the process.

Ted had cut her to the quick with his hurtful stare and derogatory accusations, but in many ways, he'd been right. And the biggest thing he'd been right about was that people were who they believed themselves to be on the inside. Eve had never particularly liked herself that way, because she'd never thought she was worthy. Worthy of the good things life seemed to bestow on so many people. Always other people, not her. The reason she'd had a closet full of bridesmaid dresses and had never been a bride had very little to do with nobody else wanting her. It had everything to do with Eve not loving herself. Well, it was time for her to change that. Eve was who she was, and she was going to own it. She was smart and caring, and she'd fight to the death for someone she loved. Her heart brimmed with understanding at the realization. Sometimes *love* meant defending. And it didn't always matter if you weren't going to get anything back. She had to do what she could while there was still time.

She stood from her desk and went to find Glenn. He was in the break room, pouring himself coffee. "I need to see that questionnaire you answered."

"What questionnaire?"

"The one from Wild West Brides. Do you still have it?"

"I downloaded it to my computer, sure."

"Can you e-mail it to me?"

He studied her and twisted his lips. "What are you going to do with it?"

"Fill it out," she said without missing a beat.

It took Eve over three hours to answer the enormously detailed questions. Some of them didn't even seem to make sense. Who cared if someone preferred whether they hung curtains or installed mini-blinds in their windows? Could the way you block out light seriously impact the success of a relationship? Glenn passed by her desk as he headed out the door. He was generally one of the last to leave.

"Don't work too late."

She gave him a weary smile. "I won't." Twenty minutes later, she was done! And also the last one left in the office. That was fine with her since she had a phone call to make, and it would be easier without any of her nosy coworkers listening. She checked the clock on the wall and saw it was nearly 7:00 p.m. That was almost 5:00 in Jackson Hole. If she was lucky, someone would still be answering at Wild West Brides. She hoped to goodness it would be Brian. She didn't believe she could take talking to Ted. Not after the huge mess she'd made of things.

Brian answered, stunned to hear from her. She had no way to know how much Ted had shared with him about their relationship, so she opted to avoid those details.

"Is this about that article you're writing?"

"Actually," she said evenly, "it is."

He waited.

"My boss here really loved it, but… I'm worried that I left out something important."

"Oh?"

"I didn't actually run a test case through your program to see how it worked myself."

Brian laughed easily. "But you did, didn't you? When you were here?"

"Yes, but that was different. Since my real goal was to write a story…"

"You weren't honestly interested in being a Wild West Bride," Brian said, getting it. There was a long pause on the line, then his voice rose with comprehension. "That's why you and Scott were a no-go from the get-go. It wasn't just because you were a reporter. Your heart wasn't in it."

"No," she admitted quietly.

"Are you telling me you know someone who is? Really interested, I mean?"

"I'm saying I know someone willing to take a chance. Take a real chance with your program to see how it works. I don't feel using my previous case as an example is really fair. Not given the reason that I came out there."

"Gotcha."

"So if you could just do me this favor and let me know the results, I'd sure appreciate it."

"I won't be able to tell you who it is," he warned. "Your match, if you've got one. You'll have to sign another participation agreement and—"

"It's not for me," she rushed in. "It's for a friend—my friend Amy. She expressed an interest. Only she's a bit shy."

"I'm not sure if I can run her profile without her permission. Does she know you're doing this for your article?"

"Yes! And she totally approves."

"Hmm."

"Please, Brian. I'm under deadline."

"What if this *friend* of yours has a match in our system?"

"That's possible, right?"

"Anything's possible. We have over eighteen hundred profiles in our database. I'm not sure you understand how popular we are. We have couples booked to come here several months out."

"If there's such a waiting list, then how did I get in last minute?"

"It was a fluke, I guess. Serendipitous. Scott was originally scheduled for October. Your profile and his were such a close match, we called and asked if he wanted to come out early."

Eve's heart sank, noting Brian had referred to *her* profile, as if he still assumed she'd submitted a legitimate one. He also clearly didn't understand the particulars of why she and Scott hadn't worked out. She guessed Ted hadn't filled him in entirely. He could have told Brian the truth and exposed Eve for who she was. But, he hadn't. He'd held her secrets in confidence. Maybe he'd been protecting her too.

"Well, if Amy gets a match. I'll pass it on to her. Let her make the call about what to do next."

"If Amy has a match, I hope you'll urge her to come out to Wyoming. It would be a shame to have another Wild West Brides near miss."

"Yes." Eve twisted a lock of hair around her finger. "So, how long will it take?"

"Well, it's a little late tonight, and I've got a rehearsal dinner to get to."

"Oh gosh, Brian! The wedding's tomorrow? Congrats!"

"Yeah, thanks." He paused a beat, apparently thinking. "The truth is this will only take a minute, and I'd hate to ask Ted to do it. I mean, you know. That might be a little…um…awkward."

So Ted *had* mentioned something about her to him. Brian at least knew there'd been something between them that hadn't worked out. Or perhaps he'd just witnessed her and Ted together and had figured it out by himself. Eve felt fire in her cheeks, hoping she was doing the right thing. Of course she was! She was trying to disprove her theory that Wild West Brides wasn't foolproof. If she did, she'd have to retract her article, or revise it at least, so it read closer to the truth.

"Besides," Brian continued, "after this weekend, I'll be out of commission awhile. Mary and I will be away on our honeymoon."

"Where're you headed?"

"Nova Scotia."

"How lovely."

"Mary loves lobster."

"Lucky girl."

"Yeah, and she'll be a miffed one if I'm late. Let me hang up here and run my numbers. I'll get back to you in a jiff."

Ten minutes later, Brian pulled some pages from his printer. Wow, this was going to be hard to tell her. Unless...? In an instant, Brian knew he was right. Eve didn't have any timid *friend* named Amy. The profile she'd submitted had been her own! He pulled Eve's original file—the one that had been matched with Scott—seeing now it couldn't possibly have been legitimate. Among other things, the woman claimed to be an expert kayaker. Brian had seen Eve on the water. That clearly wasn't her. In fact, the more he looked at these, the more he could tell that the latest profile Eve had sent was her true one. That first one had been a fake! He wondered if Ted knew about the bogus profile but understood he'd need to inform him now. Brian's lips parted in a grin as he compared Eve's real profile to that of her new match. Her perfect match. "Holy moly! What a genius I am!"

Eve paced the office, feeling like she'd been waiting forever. It had already been twenty-five minutes, and Brian had said he could run the data quickly. She thought about calling back but decided against it. Perhaps he'd run into some glitch or had decided to chuck her request altogether and go on to his rehearsal dinner. No, that didn't sound like Brian. He struck her as the sort of guy who always did what he said he was going to do.

She walked to the break room, pausing by the row of vending machines. A micro package of Milky Milanos called her, beaconing through the glass. What would it hurt to buy just one? It was already past her normal dinnertime, and her stomach was rumbling.

Eve steeled her nerves and turned away, reminding herself she'd sworn off those. *Something like matadors and cowboys.* Glenn hadn't gotten that entirely wrong. Eve walked to the coffeepot and poured herself a stale cup. Anything to take her mind off algorithms. She didn't really expect Brian to find her a match, did she? And what if he did? What would that mean next? Eve couldn't fathom flying to Wyoming to engage in another Wild West Brides adventure. She'd already done much of the program and couldn't imagine doing it again with someone else...

Eve mixed the creamer into her coffee, her emotions swirling in a murky mess. As stupid as it sounded, she missed Ted. Something had worked when they were together. And not just physically either. When she'd been with Ted, the two of them had meshed in some inexplicable way. They were at ease together, comfortable in one another's company. Well, anyhow, until that very last night. She didn't know why she was thinking about him anyway. It wasn't as if he'd spent a split second thinking of her since they'd said their good-byes. She hadn't heard a word from him.

The phone vibrated in her pocket, startling her from her reverie. She punched Answer, her hand shaking.

"Eve?" But the voice at the other end of the line wasn't Brian's.

She sucked in a gasp. "Ted."

"I was surprised to hear you called."

"It was for Brian, about the algorithms."

"So he said."

"Ted, look. I'm really sorry. About your personal information, you were right."

"What do you mean?"

"I'm not going to print it." She drew a breath, the heavy truth hitting her. "In fact, I may not print anything. Everything about this feels wrong."

"I'm glad to hear you say that. I agree."

Emotion welled in her throat, and Eve feared she'd burst out crying. "Ted, I'm so sorry. Sorry about everything. Especially the way things ended."

"I'm sorry about how things ended too."

"You what?" she asked weakly.

"We need to talk this out, set things straight. But the telephone's not the place."

Eve wasn't sure where he was headed with this, but then he told her, "I'm coming to New York."

Eve's heart lurched. "When?"

"I get in tomorrow evening. I just booked my flight."

"Before asking me?"

"I thought you'd want to hear what I've got to say."

"How can you be sure?"

"It's for your article."

Tears leaked from her eyes. "For my article, I see."

"Brian said your boss is pushing you to make this authentic. There are things you need to verify."

Eve gripped the phone in her hand and counted her measured breaths. When she got to five, she spoke. "There are."

"Then, tell me where and when, and I'll meet you. Your call."

Eve couldn't think that quickly. Her head was a jumble. The only place that came to mind was the park that was three blocks from her house. "Sunset Park. Seven o'clock."

"I'll be there."

"Okay."

"Okay, you'll be there too?"

"Yes," she said her heart breaking. Eve didn't know how she could bear to see him again and gaze in those dark brown eyes. But she had to. Needed to get this done. Finish that damn article, and say good-bye forever. If that was what this was all about. If it was about something else... No, she couldn't even dare hope that. Eve had made a wreck of everything in her life, and her relationship with Ted was no exception. There was no coming back from that now.

Chapter Twenty

Eve awoke with a jolt after having tossed and turned all night. She couldn't let that article go through. She just couldn't. Was she really in a position to diss Wild West Brides without ever having given the operation a chance herself? Who was she to argue with other people's happiness? Or with Brian's algorithms? All she knew was that Ted was coming all the way to New York to see her. That had to mean something. She just didn't know what. It hardly seemed likely he'd fly all the way here just to ream her out. Besides, he didn't sound angry on the phone. On the contrary, there was a strange calmness in his voice.

He had said he was bringing new information, though. Something to do with her article as it pertained to Wild West Brides. Or perhaps that was just a ploy to stick it to her in person. Show her firsthand that there was no match for her in the universe, in Brian's system or likely elsewhere. No, that didn't sound like Ted. Cowboy or not, he seemed a straight shooter. Eve thought back to his words in her hotel room and about how upset he'd been she'd insinuated he was a fake. She saw now she'd been unfair. Ted was who believed himself to be, and it was up to him to define that. Just as Eve defined herself by her byline, Ted did so by his Stetson. Who was Eve to argue with that?

She hurried through her morning routine and made a beeline for the train, getting to work just as Ross walked in. He was always there first. "Ross!" she said, still panting from her rush up the subway stairs. "I've got to talk to you."

He eyed her curiously in the elevator where they both stood. "What's up?"

"My article," she said between breaths. "You've got to hold it."

"The one on Wild West Brides? That's impossible. But why?"

"There've been some new developments."

He suspiciously raised an eyebrow. "Define developments."

"Ted Walker's flying to New York."

Ross let out a shrill whistle. He looked her up and down, then his eyes went wide. "Hold the phone! You can't mean? You and he…?"

"No!" she shouted. "It's not like that."

Ross shook his head. "Of course it's not. However"— he held up his index finger—"I have to admit. As the magazine's editor in chief… This does sound mighty juicy!"

"It will be worth it," she assured him, even though she wasn't certain what she was talking about herself. Either she was going to fix it so it was a fair representation of the facts in Ted's eyes, or she was going to can the article completely. She'd find a way to back out of it later, if she had to. "Just don't go to print. Not yet."

"What will we run instead?"

"That museum piece. 'Is Your Man a Michelangelo or a Picasso'?"

He giggled. "Oh yes, I recall it. Comparing major artists' masterworks to in-the-sack styles. Quite cute, that one."

"It will work," Eve said. "I guarantee it."

"Fine, fine." He studied her. "What's in it for you?"

She beamed up at him, but any confidence was feigned. "A better article, I hope."

"That's my girl!" He flashed her a happy smile. "I knew I'd picked right with you."

Ted stared at his best friend in the world. "I hate to leave you like this. On the day of your wedding."

"Come on, man! You're only missing the reception. You're here for the morning nuptials. That's the part that counts."

"I'm going to have to make a quick exit right after the *I dos*."

Brian grinned broadly. "I know. I did the math."

"You really think I'm doing the right thing?"

"You're asking *me*? Computer genius extraordinaire?"

For the past twelve hours, Ted had been all bluster and bravado. Now suddenly he found himself losing his nerve. "What if she doesn't want to see me?"

"She's already meeting you at Sunset Park!"

"Yeah, but what if it rains, or—"

"Will you listen to yourself? Man up! Put on your boots and spurs if you have to."

Ted glanced down at his tuxedo. "No time to change before the plane."

"Even better. *That*," he said, eying his best friend's outfit, "makes a statement."

"What kind of statement?"

"You can take the cowboy out of the Stetson, but you can't take the cowboy out of the cowboy."

"You just made that crap up."

"Yeah, maybe." Brian adjusted his bow tie in the mirror, then turned toward Ted, looking serious. "Listen, man." He gripped Ted by the shoulders. "All you've done these past four weeks is talk about her. You might not have told me she faked her profile, but you sure as heck indicated she'd faked falling for you. All this time, you've been moping around. Feeling sorry for yourself. Wondering how you could have misjudged her. But what if you didn't?

What if Eve really is who you thought she was in the beginning?"

"What do you mean?"

"Someone you could spend the rest of your life with?"

Ted's mouth hung open. "I never thought that!"

Brian smirked and tilted his chin. "Liar."

"What?"

"I saw the way you watched her that day, the day she nearly fell off her horse. Heck, I'll bet you couldn't even force yourself to take your eyes off her on the trail ride. And that was back when she was paired with Scott!"

Ted swallowed hard.

"Then I saw you together up at Jenny Lake *and* at the river. You weren't pretending and neither was she. That, my man, was the real deal."

Ted threw out his hands. "So what am I supposed to do?"

"I thought you had a plan?"

"I have a pocket full of algorithms."

Brian patted his shoulder. "That's a start."

"Brian…"

"Ted!"

"What?"

"Will you shut up already and let me be the man of the hour? It's almost showtime."

"Oh right. Sorry."

On their way out the door, Brian shot him a wink. "Kind of cool to think the next show might be yours."

"Bite your tongue."

"Bite *me*." Brian wrapped an arm around him. "Trust me. It's going to be all right."

Meanwhile, in Manhattan, Eve forced herself through her day, trying to focus on anything other than what would come at the end of it. Ted Walker was coming to see her! Who on earth could explain that? Maybe Brian could, she thought with a hum. The truth was Brian had never gotten back to her after she'd submitted "Amy's" information. Was Ted coming to admonish her for that? Say she'd had no business tinkering further with the inner workings of Wild West Brides?

No, that didn't seem right. Ted could have just as easily told her that on the phone. But why was he coming to New York? Traveling all that way? That hardly seemed necessary just to scold her. Eve felt the back of her neck flash hot and had the instinct to pile up her hair. She picked up the pen from Wild West Brides but set it down—opting for a chopstick instead. She always saved the extras after she and Glenn ordered takeout for lunch.

"You seem a little off today," Glenn said, leaning into her desk. "Everything all right?"

Eve shocked Glenn by grabbing him by his lapels. "He's coming!"

"Who is?"

"Ted!" she grated under her breath. "Tonight."

"Wow. Are you telling me that you and he...? He and you...? Get out of town!"

"Glenn," she hissed. "Keep your voice down."

"Right, right." He angled closer. "So what was it like? Riding... I mean, riding with a real cow—"

She slapped his chest. "None of your business!"

Glenn's face reddened. "That good, huh? Well, it's a good thing he's coming to catch up."

"That's not why he's coming," she whispered back. "He's coming to talk."

"Sure, he is." There was a mysterious glint in Glenn's eyes.

"What does that mean?"

"Eve." He heaved a sigh. "How many men that you know travel nearly two thousand miles just to talk?"

She thought about this. "Not a lot, I guess."

"Practically not any," he assured her. "Best be prepared to listen up, girlfriend. That cowboy's got something to say."

Ted reached Sunset Park at twilight. He found Eve on a bench at a high crest on the hill overlooking the East River. It faced Manhattan's skyline, the Statue of Liberty lording over the waters between the banks of the financial district and Brooklyn. She looked up as he approached, deep red curls playing about her shoulders. Ted's heart bounded. Eve was even more beautiful than he remembered.

He hurried to reach her growing uncomfortable in the summer heat beneath his warm attire. "You're in a tuxedo?" she asserted with surprise. Those were the first words from her lips. Not, *Where's your cowboy hat?* Or even, *It's nice to see you.*

"Brian got married this morning," he explained. He came and took a seat beside her on the bench overlooking the water. Below them, children played an impromptu game of soccer. Farther away, others flew kites.

Little worry lines creased her brow, and it was all Ted could do not to reach out and smooth them. "I hope you didn't miss his wedding."

"I was there," he assured her. "But there wasn't much time before my flight." He indicated his clothing, and she immediately understood. Ted had gone straight from the ceremony to the plane.

"You didn't have to rush," she told him. "We could have waited."

Her eyes were lovely in the sunset, a deep russet brown. "No, Eve. This couldn't wait." He slipped his hand into his coat pocket and pulled out some papers.

"What's this?"

"Algorithms." He shot her a quirky smile. "Yours, it seems. And mine. Assuming you're really *Amy.*"

Eve drew a breath, clearly seeing there was no point in denying it. "I am." Her eyes were full of apology. "I'm sorry I lied to Brian, I just needed to know that—"

"Wild West Brides is for real?"

"Yes."

"It is, Eve. More than you know." He handed over his papers. "Take a minute. Look at these."

She stared at his name on a page. "But what were you doing in the system? Did you just put your data in?"

"It's been there," he told her. "Way back from the beginning, guinea-pig stage. It was so long ago, I'd honestly forgotten my profile was in there. Brian had too. It's not like it's ever pulled a match before."

He met her eyes. "Until now."

Eve scanned through their answers, her mouth hanging open as she compared their forms, page by page. "This can't be right. On the outside, we're so different, but here on paper... The way we answered these questions... Most of our answers are the same."

"And the ones that aren't identical are answered in compatible ways," Ted said. "Eve," he continued. "I want you to know this never happens. Even at Wild West Brides, this sort of match is extremely rare. Brian and I have never seen it before."

"Not even with Brian and Mary?"

"Not even."

She dropped the papers on her lap.

"It's no mistake that we're a match. Brian's algorithms are never wrong."

"So this all boils down to that?" she asked with hurt in her voice. "Some set of math problems? If I hadn't called Brian yesterday evening, you wouldn't be sitting here now?"

"That's not true." He met her gaze and spoke from the heart, hoping his wouldn't fail him. "I've been thinking about us for a long time. Ever since you left."

Her chin trembled as she spoke. "I've been thinking about you too. Ted…" She drew a breath. "I know I screwed up with the article, and I'm sorry. I went in and tried to fix it, but I'm afraid I only made it worse."

"Worse than calling me a counterfeit cowboy?"

"Actually, I took that part out." Her gaze was sincere. "Any mention of your parents too."

"Rebecca?"

"History."

"You can say that again." He studied her in the twilight. "Just what are you telling me?"

She dropped her chin. "I kind of put in something about a jilted bride."

"A what?"

When she met his gaze again, her eyes were moist. "It was me, Ted. It was *all about me* in the worst possible way."

"What happened to this girl? This jilted bride?"

Eve shrugged as a tear escaped her. "I guess her story's still being written."

Ted reached over and gently stroked her cheek. "Sounds like that story needs revising."

She sobbed softly. "Maybe."

Ted cupped her chin in his hand. "Hey, nothing's gone to print, has it?"

Eve shook her head.

"Then there's still time."

"For what?"

"To write a happy ending." He held her bleary gaze. "I don't know what happened in Wyoming, but I know it was good. When the two of us were together, everything felt right. I want to feel that way again. Like we did out at Jenny Lake when we were..."

"Together," she whispered.

A lump rose in Ted's throat, but he pushed the words past it. "I know you're in New York and I'm in Jackson Hole, but..." His voice cracked, and he stopped, fighting the sting in his eyes. "I want us to start over. Really get to know each other. Because, you know, I think there's something good here. Something worth keeping." He looked at her, pleading. "Please say you agree?"

"Is that why you flew to New York? Because you want to..." She paused on the word. "Date me?"

He took her hand. "Algorithms are great. But at the end of the day, they're just math on paper, like you say." He looked deep in her eyes, knowing her soulful expression reflected his. "But darling, hearts don't lie." He trusted his wasn't lying to him now, because all it told him to do was take her in his arms. Her eyes were warm, welcoming...brilliant in the sunset.

"No they don't, cowboy."

He pulled her up against him, holding her close.

"Tell me that means yes."

"Yes, Ted. Oh yes. I'm open to that. Definitely open. I've got a Wild West Brides pen by my calendar. You can have any date you want."

"I want as many of them as I can get."

"They're yours," she said in a breathy whisper.

"Oh yeah? All three hundred and sixty-five of them?"

"Yeah."

Ted grinned and lowered his mouth to hers.

"Yee-haw."

Epilogue

Ten months later, Eve stood with Ted on a Wyoming mountaintop. He was taking her paragliding for the first time. He patted her hand with his as he snuggled behind her, their harnesses buckled tight. A gorgeous solitaire shone on her left hand. He'd placed it there just last Tuesday, when he'd asked her to be his bride up at Jenny Lake. When she'd said yes, she'd felt like the luckiest woman alive.

"Just remember what I taught you, and you'll do fine." His voice was husky over her shoulder, and Eve trembled. The wind was picking up, and they were soon to be airborne. But with Ted keeping her in his arms, she knew she'd be safe. Eve always felt safe with Ted around, no matter their adventure. These past ten months had been a whirlwind of fun. She'd gotten to know Jackson Hole in winter and had learned how to downhill ski. While she wasn't the best outdoorswoman, Ted was a very patient teacher. With his guidance, she'd tackled things she'd never believed herself capable of doing, and she'd loved every minute.

The Wild West Brides article she'd finally published had won her plenty of attention at the magazine and earned her the admiration of Ted's parents besides. They'd said she was a fabulous writer and were so pleased with the way she'd profiled their son and his booming business. They'd told her this at Thanksgiving, when Ted had taken her home to meet his brothers and the rest of the Walker clan. They'd all accepted Eve warmly and had greeted the news of their engagement with shouts of delight. She could still practically hear those congrats ringing out of Ted's cell phone receiver.

She and Ted weren't the only ones on course for a happy ending. Shortly after they reconciled, Eve had gone to meet with Glenn's cousin Debbie to explain the situation with Scott. Debbie had been horrified her information had been used without her permission and had insisted on sending Scott an apology. Once Ted cleared it with Scott that he was okay to receive her e-mail, she wrote him, and they began an online correspondence. A few months later, they spoke on the phone. Last month, Scott flew to Manhattan. Soon, Debbie would head to Montana to see his world and meet his little girl. Who knew where things would go from there? Brian's algorithms were never wrong.

"Just let the wind take us," Ted said, urging Eve forward. "It will be fun." They started to run in small springy steps.

"Fun! Right!" She tried not to let her nerves show but knew they were natural. Didn't Ted always say that a little bit of fear indicated a healthy self-preservationist attitude? "I think I'll just focus on meeting Brian and Mary for drinks later."

"Darling," he said with a growl, "I've got other plans for us later."

"Stop it!" she said, swatting his hand. "You're just trying to distract me." Suddenly, she realized it had worked! Her feet were no longer on the ground, and they were soaring! "Ooohhh, oh my gosh!"

"No problem, sweetheart." He drew an arm around her waist. "I've got you."

"I'm not sure I can do this."

Ted bellowed a laugh. "You already are!"

That's right! She was! Who would have believed it! She, Eve Parker, was doing something so daring! Then again, she always felt daring around Ted. Just looking in his eyes made her heart race and her head go all woozy. Each and every time.

"It's only going to get better, you know!" he called above the winds.

She caught her breath at the beauty of the valley below, where the Snake River curved beneath them. Up ahead, the Teton Range spiked in a clear blue sky. "The view?"

He tightened his arms around her. "I was talking about you and me."

Eve knew it was true. She couldn't possibly be any happier. It was like she was on top of the world, and the rest of the earth was down below. She giggled aloud at the thought.

"What's so funny?"

"I just had a literal moment."

"I'm really glad you decided to do this with me."

"I am too."

"Eve?" he asked above the wind's roar. "Still think I'm a fake?"

"Oh no, honey," she said with a laugh. "I know you're the real thing."

"How about I prove that to you later?"

"That would be your pleasure."

"And yours," he teased.

"Shut up and enjoy the view."

"I've got everything I need right here," he said, holding her close.

The End

Related Characters

Some of the characters mentioned in *Counterfeit Cowboy* appear in other Ginny Baird stories. North Carolina artist Gweldolyn Marsh meets handsome rancher Dan Holbrook in *Santa Fe Fortune.* Eve Parker is first introduced as Jessica Bloom's best friend in *How to Marry a Matador* when Jess wakes up accidentally married to sexy Spaniard Fernando Garcia de la Vega. If you'd like to learn more about these novels, you'll find the description and first chapter from each included next. Happy reading!

SANTA FE FORTUNE
Some things are worth more than money...

North Carolina artist Gwendolyn Marsh is on a New Mexico mission. She's got ten days to raise twenty thousand dollars in cash. In financial straits herself and hoping to help her sister, Gwen's determined to bring monetary relief fast. What Gwen doesn't bank on is getting the utterly handsome and irresistible Dan Holbrook in the bargain. Still recovering from a failed first marriage, Gwen's not sure she'll ever love again. Can a midnight ride in the desert convince her to change her mind?

Billionaire bachelor Dan Holbrook is an outdoorsy man who knows how to behave in polite company. So when his sister Nancy asks him to run her Santa Fe gallery while she's away, Dan thinks he'll have no trouble manning the store. That is, until Ms. Gwendolyn Marsh blows into town like a wild, west wind, upending his world with her womanly ways. Dan's heart hasn't healed from its last disaster. Can he risk opening himself up to hurt a second time?

Santa Fe Fortune

"I had a really great time tonight," she said, beaming up at him and feeling very much as if it had been a date.

"Me too," he said, stepping a fraction of an inch closer. Sea-blue eyes washed over her, threatening to pull her under. And boy, did she want to get swept away. "I'm glad you agreed to see me tomorrow, even if it's just an arrangement."

Gwen sensed Dan could rearrange her heart every which way, if she wasn't careful. "I'm glad I'm seeing you too," she said, feeling the warmth in her cheeks.

"Ten o'clock work for you?" he asked, his tone growing gravelly.

"Uh-huh," she uttered, mesmerized by his gaze.

He moved nearer now, his mouth just inches away. "I'll be damned if I don't want to kiss you," he said, his voice a husky rasp.

And she'd be damned if she didn't want him to. "Dan…" she said, tilting up her chin and closing her eyes.

"But I won't," he said, snapping her back to attention, eyes open. "Not now. Not here. Not like this…"

She started to speak as he brought his fingers to her lips. "If ever I've seen a woman who deserves to be kissed well, it's you. But the timing has got to be right. You have to be sure." He cast a cursory glance at her wedding band and backed away. "I need to be sure. Something tells me we've both gone down a path neither of us wants to travel again…"

Chapter One

Gwendolyn Marsh leaned across the large oak table that served as a desk. "I'm going to be honest with you, Mr. Holbrook. I didn't fly all the way out here to get swindled." Dan stared in disbelief at the incredibly contentious woman. *Swindled* was an awfully big accusation coming from such a small frame. She couldn't stand more than five foot five in heels, and she'd nearly tumbled off them striding into the place.

"Like I told you, Mrs. Marsh, I'm not in the position to make that decision. If two thousand a canvas is what Ms. Holstein quoted you in the email, then I'm afraid I'll need to stick by that."

Soft gold curls fell at uneven angles, framing a lovely face as deep brown eyes homed in on him. If she weren't so hard-edged, he might consider her beautiful. Dan stopped himself, realizing appraisals of the clientele weren't in his job description.

"It's *Ms.,* if you must know."

Some lucky fellow was off the hook.

"My apologies. I saw the wedding band and…"

"It's a relic, okay? I haven't gotten used to going without it."

"I'm sorry, I had no idea. I understand it takes a while."

She leveled him a look, as if he were the culprit. Hey, maybe in her eyes, all men were. Dan had met the type before and could easily read the signs: *steer clear, not for you buddy, a sexy woman's not everything…* Sexy? Did he just think *sexy?* Gwendolyn Marsh wasn't movie star thin like most females here. Her formfitting sundress hugged every curve in just the right way. Wrong way, as far as he was concerned. This was just another sign he'd been alone too long. It wasn't like Dan didn't have his reasons. In fact, when he was being honest, Dan realized he was likely worse news for her than she was for him. All women after a while had hopes, dreams…and Dan Holbrook was just the man to dash them.

Dark eyes sparked with fierce determination. "I think I'd like to speak to Ms. Holstein myself."

"I'm afraid that won't be possible."

She arched one perfectly manicured eyebrow. "Why not?"

This was just what Dan needed, a hot-tempered, hot-bodied woman waltzing into his Santa Fe gallery on a hot July afternoon. Okay, it wasn't technically his gallery…

Dan cursed himself for his soft spot in agreeing to run the place while Nancy was away. He didn't even like being indoors.

"Ms. Holstein is in the south of France, will be until next month."

She pulled her naturally plump lips into a thin pink line. "I see." She faltered slightly, nearly losing her composure. There was sheen to her eyes that made them look moist. Dan hoped she wasn't about to break down crying. Nancy had assured him this would be easy, just a few clients flying in from out of state. Surprise negotiations and weepy women weren't in the mix. Negotiations Dan could handle. Weepy women were another story.

A bell tinkled above the door, and a couple of well-dressed patrons entered, a man in an expensive suit and a woman wearing a tailored dress and high-end cowgirl boots.

"Be right with you folks," Dan told them, surmising these were the buyers from Los Angeles.

Gwen stood, apparently taking this as a dismissal. "Well, I guess that's it, then." She tucked her clutch under one arm and thrust forward the opposite hand. "Thanks for your time."

Dan sent a furtive glance at the Californians perusing shelves of New Mexican pottery and pretending not to listen. "Ms. Marsh, I'm afraid we got off on the wrong..." She tapped a strappy sandal, sporting bright painted nails and multiple toe rings. Heat rose at Dan's nape as his gaze eased up shapely legs. "...foot."

She withdrew her hand and cocked her head sideways, waiting.

"What I mean is, please sit back down, and let's discuss this like reasonable people. I'm sure we can work something out." Dan cringed at the sound of his own voice. Groveling? Here was a word not even in his vocabulary, yet he was being just about as placating as humanly possible. Dan wasn't doing it for himself, he remembered. He was doing this for Nancy. Other than the day-to-day oversight of things, which really was no problem, she'd given him only two jobs to do. Surely a man as capable at cutting deals as he was wouldn't have trouble selling a few items to some Los Angeles industry execs and buying canvases from an easy-going North Carolina native. Dan had a notion Nancy had never met Gwendolyn Marsh face-to-face when she'd made the latter assessment.

The hardness lining her eyes eased just a little. "I suppose I could stay for a bit," she said, her voice taking on the lilt of the mid-Atlantic South. She took her seat, splaying the lap of her flowered sundress across tightly nestled knees.

The Californians tastefully removed themselves to the back of the gallery to study a photographic desert landscape series, and Dan sat as well. He plucked a hanky from his suit pocket and dabbed the back of his neck, thinking it had to be over a hundred degrees in here.

Something tender welled in Dan's throat, and he realized he wasn't just doing this for Nancy. For some inexplicable reason, he felt driven to be nice to Ms. Marsh for her own sake. Never mind that she'd practically bulldozed right over him crashing in here. After all, he'd dealt with worse in business before. The truth was Nancy had given him some leeway. If Marsh really pushed, Dan could go up as high as three thousand a pop, mostly because Nancy had faith in Marsh's work and thought it was good. Nancy also believed that Marsh could develop a Santa Fe following. Many of the buyers here came from the West Coast, and Marsh's oils capturing snippets of sea life would be a ready sell. Dan had seen the slides, and they were impressive. Borrowing more from impressionism than realism, Marsh had a way of zeroing in on the smallest, seemingly inconsequential detail, like an isolated seashell, and illuminating it in a special and grandiose way.

She opened her purse and withdrew a thin ledger. "If you'd let me show you my figures, I'm sure you'll understand why my prices have gone up."

Dan scanned the haphazardly arranged numbers, deciding she was no mathematician. He pointed to one clumsily assumed total. "I can understand where material costs have climbed, but how exactly is it that your hourly rate has doubled?"

"Hard times, Mr. Holbrook," she said without flinching. "Don't you read the papers?"

"*Wall Street Journal* and you?" he bantered without skipping a beat.

"Well, I…read, of course." With that, she awkwardly angled an elbow and sent her clutch crashing to the floor. "Oh no!"

A small cloud of makeup powder-puffed up from beneath them as a rolling lipstick assaulted Dan's loafer. To this day, he'd never understood the mysteries of a woman's bag.

"Here, let me," he began.

"No! I've got it!"

They bent simultaneously toward the mound of sprawled purse contents, nearly knocking heads. "I'm sorry!" he said, down on hands and knees to help her.

"My fault!"

A scent overtook him as cunning and fine as the most succulent desert flower. Dan looked up into bewitching brown eyes less than six inches away. Whatever was happening here, he had to put a halt to it. This was no sensible way for a man pushing forty to behave. He was reeling like a raving teenager. He hadn't been in a position this compromising with a woman in a while, and it showed. All sorts of crazy thoughts went racing through his head, like how it might feel to kiss her good and hard as she probably deserved.

"You guys okay over there?" a pair of cowgirl boots called from the corner.

"Thanks, we've got it!" Gwen replied, scooting back on her knees. She couldn't believe this mess! What had she gotten herself into? Here she was with this hunky beast of a man, trapped beneath a solid yet decorative desk.

He had a rugged face, tanned like he was used to working outdoors. His sandy hair held a hint of sunlight too. Toned muscles strained beneath his suit jacket as he posed on all fours, looking far more like a predator in the wild than a staid art collector. Gwen had an improbable instinct to flee but was powerless to run away. He'd been an impossible man above board, but down here in the shadows, he revealed something more. Instinct told Gwen that Holbrook was the sort of man who knew how to kiss a woman and kiss her right. She imagined getting swept into his powerful arms, his mouth moving down on hers…

"Are you all right?" His gaze dove into her as heat crept up her cheeks.

"Yes, fine. That's all, I think," she said, scooping the remainders into her clutch.

Gwen didn't know why his gorgeous stare had unnerved her so. It wasn't like she was attracted to him, for heaven's sake. If her take on Holbrook was correct, he had plenty of women falling all over him already. What would a sophisticated Western entrepreneur like him want with a Carolina girl like her anyway? Apart from a quick good time, probably not a lot, and Gwendolyn Marsh was quite done with being somebody's goodtime girl, thank you very much.

Little lines pulled at the corners of his mouth, and she realized suddenly they were still both on the floor. "If you've got all you need, don't you think we should…" He gave a thumbs-up, and she pushed back, standing awkwardly.

Holbrook brushed off his trousers, the slight tugs showing off powerfully muscled thighs. Clearly not just a gallery owner, she thought, cheeks flaming as he caught her staring.

A tense moment ensued as both appeared to forget where they were or what they were there for. As if to remind them, the California man loudly cleared his throat.

"Just finishing up," Dan told him. "Ms. Marsh," he began, addressing her.

"Gwen, please. I'd be happy if you called me Gwen." She smoothed the wrinkles from her dress and straightened the neckline.

"Gwen," he said, offering up his first true smile since she'd arrived, and boy, was it a winner. If a heartbreaker contest existed in all of the Southwest, Gwen would bet on Holbrook to take the prize. "I'm afraid I've already taken up too much of your time."

Gwen spied the California couple circling closer like sharks, apparently having grown tired of waiting, and panic set in. What a terrible two days she'd had. First, her flight to Atlanta was delayed. Then, she'd missed her Albuquerque connection, causing her to miss her originally scheduled gallery appointment. To top it off, when she finally got a replacement flight, she'd chipped a nail stuffing her bulging carry-on into the overhead compartment.

Making Santa Fe from the airport last night was easy. Finding the craftily concealed entity of Holbrook and Holstein on Canyon Road this morning proved more elusive. Even her GPS was miffed, telling her to make legal U-turns wherever possible, no matter that the prospect involved going round and round in the Vegan Market parking lot.

Now, after making a wreck of this business call, she'd be leaving here having done no business at all. Not one sale to the gallery, despite her tumultuous flight and anxiety-producing encounter with Dan Holbrook.

Gwen pulled herself up a little straighter and squared her small shoulders. She couldn't leave New Mexico without getting what she came for. Too many people depended on her, and this was the one shot she had.

"Maybe we can continue this conversation later?" she asked with a hopeful twist to her lips.

"I was just about to suggest that."

"You were?" she asked with surprise.

"Ms. Marsh…" He stopped himself. "Gwen… Do you really think Holbrook and Holstein would have had you come all this way if we didn't have a genuine interest in your work?" Crinkles formed at the corners of his blue eyes, and Gwen's heart soared.

"But I thought you said the prices quoted to me in the email were…"

"Everything in life is negotiable. Well, almost everything. Tell you what, why don't you give me a few hours to put through a phone call to France, and I'll see what I can do."

In an instant, Gwen retracted every uncharitable thought she'd had about him. When she'd first walked into the swanky, upscale warehouse and spied him double-checking the pricing on a large wall weaving, she'd imagined him incredibly stuck-up. Who wouldn't be with that six-foot build and well-proportioned frame that spoke of power and unerring self-control? She'd pegged him as the rigid sort who never took no for an answer and considered his own words the final determinant. Now that he was showing a small sliver of humanity, she realized she might have misjudged him.

"I'd love to talk again," she said, meaning it sincerely. "When's best for you?"

"How about tomorrow at lunch? Will that work?"

Ms. Holstein, his business partner, Gwen presumed, had proposed that Gwen make a little vacation out of her stay in Santa Fe while she was at it. Her sister Marian had thought it was a fine idea too. *"Go for it, Gwen! Now's your chance to finally get away!"* What Marian didn't know, and Gwen hadn't been prepared to tell her, was that Gwen's coming to Santa Fe had a whole lot to do with her.

"I'm booked at the inn for ten days," she said, smiling softly. "So, lunch tomorrow is fine."

Holbrook surprised her with a smile of his own. "Awesome." He nabbed a gallery card and quickly penned something on the back. "Let's meet here. Something tells me the conversation might flow a little better between us given a couple of avocado margaritas."

"Avocado?" she retorted, half stunned, half horrified.

Holbrook gave a genuine chuckle as she accepted his card. "Nobody's forcing the hard stuff on you. I'm sure there will be tea and soda available too."

There was a twinkle in his eye that set her tailbone tingling. Slow down there, sister, Gwen told herself. This is strictly business now. Not anywhere near a date.

"What time?" she asked primly, pinning her clutch to her side.

He studied her in an amused way. "One o'clock okay?"

"One sounds fine!" she said, scurrying toward the exit before she could do or say something absurd.

"Watch the...!"

Gwen spun toward him, noting she'd nearly upset a pretty, handblown glass vase with the edge of her bag. She grimaced, slinking out the door as the gaping Californians gawked on.

Once outside and beyond sight of the gallery's windows, Gwen snatched her bag from beneath her arm and whacked herself soundly on the forehead. Stupid, stupid, stupid. She might have blown the whole thing. And not just by breaking a priceless piece of art. The way she'd started things out had been nothing short of shameless. Crafting a confrontation with the primary gallery owner. Clearly, that could lead to nothing but butting heads.

Gwen felt a warmth surge through her, recalling their close encounter of the nearly carnal kind. There was more to Dan Holbrook than met the eye. Hadn't he just proved that with his turn of kindness at the end? But the truth of the matter was that whatever sort of man he was, or wasn't, was beside the point. Gwen had come to Santa Fe on a mission, and that mission involved dollar signs. She didn't just want the money; she needed it. Twenty thousand in cash, and she wasn't leaving New Mexico without it.

Dan finished business quickly with the couple from Los Angeles after offering sincere apologies for making them wait. They'd prearranged to purchase the desert photo series, and everything, including price negotiations, thank goodness, had been settled with Nancy in advance. It was a simple matter of the pair presenting a check and Dan providing the receipt. In the morning, he'd arrange for shipping, and Nancy's gallery assistant would be in to help with the details. That would be the simple part of Dan's day. Lunchtime could prove more problematic.

Dan chided himself for suggesting Gwen meet him at La Cantina rather than here. Outwardly, he told himself that he was being charitable. Gwen had seemed so uptight at the gallery, perhaps a more comfortable venue would be less intimidating. He'd read her résumé and understood that if she sold through Holbrook and Holstein, it would be her first real sale, her official launch in the art world. But deep in the veiled recesses of his soul, Dan suspected a slight ulterior motive. He hadn't enjoyed the company of an attractive woman in ages, and this was a safe way to do it. Lunch in the middle of the day, a straightforward business deal? What could be more innocent? Raw doubts niggled at him as he warned himself against getting in too deep. The way he'd sprung the invitation on Gwen had been completely out of character. It had been a split-second decision, an act on impulse, and Dan was anything but an impulsive man.

He would never have built his empire of custom-design homes for the moneyed set if he'd operated from a basis of anything but collected cool. In those circles, Dan was known for his keen eye and level head, as well as his effectiveness in putting together a team. From the highest-level architect to the most basic yet very skilled carpenter, every one of Holbrook Designs' workers was treated with utmost respect and handsomely paid. This was particularly appreciated in the current economic climate but had always been the operational mode for Dan. Whether times were easy or hard, Dan's business remained steady. While his homes certainly weren't cheap, they were of a consistent quality the buyer could count on. Plus, Dan was a man of his word who stood by his product. People could depend on him to deliver the best and ensure they had a comfortable and stunningly beautiful place in which to live for years to come. It was an area in which Dan felt confident, competent.

This temporary gallery running made him feel something altogether different, and Dan didn't like it one bit. While working with the California couple had gone fine, dealing with Ms. Gwendolyn Marsh had thrown him unexpectedly off-kilter. Nancy had nowhere near prepared him for that. Just because he'd helped his big sister finance this place, that didn't mean he wanted to be involved in any intimate way. Nancy was the art history major who loved the ins and outs of acquiring art. Running a gallery in Santa Fe had always been her dream, and once Dan had found himself in a position to help with that, he'd been more than happy to foot the bill. He'd never imagined that she'd repay him by listing his name as the primary gallery owner. This perpetually led to confusion, like during his exchange with Gwen today.

No matter. He'd straighten all that out tomorrow. Surely, after a good lunch and some cordial conversation, they'd arrive at a fair compromise on price. It would be a simple matter to smooth over during coffee and dessert. Then Ms. Gwendolyn Marsh could cart her sexy little tail all the way back to North Carolina, and Dan would continue counting down the days to Nancy's return, when he would once again be free to retreat to the peaceful quiet of Paradise Ranch. Life wasn't really so complicated after all, Dan decided, thinking it through. All you needed was a plan. And Dan's plans didn't include one firecracker of a Southern belle upending his world and sending his foolish heart racing. For Dan Holbrook, days like that were done. His throat ached at the memory. He swallowed hard, trying to force it back down. Dan had stepped into the fire once and had come out barbequed. No need to start poking at coals again.

Gwen sat on the patio of her airy suite, surrounded by sweeping adobe walls, potted ferns, and cactus flowers. Despite the record-high temperatures, the lack of humidity made it pleasant enough to stay outdoors in the shade. She sipped at her host's complimentary glass of chardonnay, knowing she needed to be cautious. At seven thousand feet above sea level, one glass of wine could feel like two. The inn's cocktail hour had also offered a selection of fruits, vegetables, and cheeses, and Gwen had fixed herself a small plate as a buffering against the booze. She'd have to remain mindful of herself tomorrow at lunch, particularly in light of the proposed margaritas.

Gwen couldn't help but feel a slight tingle of hopeful anticipation. For the first time in as long as she remembered, she'd be eating out with an eligible man. She knew, of course, that it was just an art deal, and she was merely passing through town. It was nonetheless hard to deny the tiniest fluttering in her tummy that sprang to life each time she recalled being face-to-face on the floor with the undeniably handsome Holbrook. Had something authentic actually passed between them, or had Gwen been so nervous and delusional as to have imagined the whole thing?

She glanced down at the simple gold band on her left ring finger. Gwen wasn't sure if it was her marriage she couldn't forget or her failure to maintain it. *"Marshes aren't quitters!"* her mom, Elizabeth, had always said. While life may have quit on Elizabeth, she wasn't about to let her daughters give up on anything. It was a mantra burned into them, her and her sister Marian both. Gwen only wished Marian had quit having babies about three children ago. Marian was expecting her sixth, and after years of verbal and physical abuse, her alcoholic husband, Tom, had finally run out on her. Gwen had truthfully considered this a blessing, as it had been clear after the first couple of years that Marian never intended to leave Tom.

Marian worked part-time as a hospital nurse and tried to get the day shift as much as possible. When she was gone, she left her oldest, the eleven-year-old, in charge. During night shifts, her elderly neighbor, Ms. Tilly, helped out. During the academic year, Marian had daycare arranged for the twins while the others were in school. She wasn't sure how she'd manage once the new baby came along, especially under the threat of losing her home. Marian's mortgage was several months overdue, and the collectors were moving in. She hadn't told Gwen that Tom stopped sending payments, or that she was in so deep, until it was almost too late. As it was, Marian barely had funds in her meager savings account to buy a few months' worth of diapers. Her checking account was essentially empty, being worn down month after month by her family's needs, including the kids' doctors' bills.

Marian had been in tears when she'd told Gwen the truth. If she lost her house, she feared her children would be taken away from her. She had nowhere else to go. Gwen's sparse two-bedroom could scarcely hold them all, not for any length of time, at least. And their mom, having long ago been placed in the memory-care unit of a retirement home, was far from being able to help. She barely scraped by on Social Security and most days didn't recognize either of her daughters, besides.

If Marian could just hang on one more year until the twins were in school, she thought she could make it. With only the new baby to place in daycare, she'd be able to work full-time. That would give her benefits like a retirement pension and health insurance. She'd be better able to meet her kids' medical expenses as well as plan for her own future. As it stood, she had six months of back mortgage to pay and another twelve months' obligation to look forward to. She was overwhelmed and in pieces, unsure of what to do. Taking Tom to court wasn't an option. Marian didn't have the financial resources, and even if she did, it would be hard squeezing blood from a stone. Tom was on and off the bottle and in and out of work. She couldn't rely on him now any more than she had during their marriage.

It was a dire and depressing situation. Gwen had thought for weeks about what she might do to help her sister. The trouble was Gwen was in financial strife herself. Robert had been so furious at her for kicking him out, he'd run up over ten thousand dollars in credit-card debt on purpose. The pro bono women's shelter attorney Gwen consulted said there was nothing Gwen could do about Robert maxing out the account jointly held in their names.

Gwen was unfortunately just as liable for half of his debts as entitled to half of his earnings. Good luck with that. Robert, a successful production assistant with a Hollywood company providing East Coast sets, had found plenty of loopholes in which to stash his cash. Gwen twisted the simple wedding band once, realizing her cheeks were damp.

She finished off her chardonnay, more determined than ever to sell those canvases and at the best possible price. She'd started small with a few local juried art shows around town, then had dared to put a modest portfolio of slides together and began sending it out. Holbrook and Holstein in Santa Fe had been her first real nibble. In effect, it had been a really big bite. Top dollar for her work, plus the cost of round-trip air tickets and accommodations to boot. Holbrook probably thought that Gwen was being greedy, trying to barter up the price for her own gain. Nothing could be further from the truth. Marian's kids needed their mama, and Gwen needed to help her baby sister. One way or another, Gwen was going to see this through. Dan Holbrook could think anything about her that he liked. She'd never see him again after tomorrow anyway.

End of sample from Santa Fe Fortune.

HOW TO MARRY A MATADOR
Was it really a mistake?

New York telecommunications expert Jessica Bloom has never quite gotten things right. She's failed at relationships, and only believes herself to have moved ahead at work due to dumb luck. Her fortunes change when she flies to Madrid on an acquisitions deal -- but wakes up married to a matador instead! While she's held a burning attraction to her handsome business adversary for months, she never dreamed she'd make such an enormous split-second decision. Surely, this is a mistake they can both get undone? Her new husband, however, has plans to the contrary...

Fernando Garcia de la Vega runs a telecommunications firm poised for a US takeover. What Fernando doesn't expect, is its beautiful International Division head also capturing his heart. Descended from a long line of bullfighters, Fernando stands to inherit the family's lucrative estate, if he meets the criteria in his grandfather's will and marries by age thirty-two. Yet, a marriage of convenience was something Fernando was loathe to consider... until now. When the fates conspire to put the right woman in the right place -- at the right time, how can Fernando deny his destiny? His only problem lies in convincing Jessica to remain his bride.

How to Marry a Matador

Fernando sighed, worry lines creasing his brow. "You're terribly angry with me, aren't you?"

"It takes two to tango, Fernando. I'm not saying all of this is your fault. I played a part in what happened yesterday too."

He turned toward her with a penetrating look. "That's what I don't understand. Why did you?"

Jess felt a lurch of emotion as he dissected her with his earnest green gaze. "I...don't know."

He leaned toward her with a husky whisper. "Oh, but I think you do."

He drew nearer, his mouth hovering over hers. Jess cursed herself for so badly wanting his kiss. His kisses had been so tantalizing last night, they'd made her lose all sense of reason. And it wasn't just the way he'd held her. When he'd looked deep in her eyes and said that one thing, she'd inexplicably believed him as she had no man before.

"Why did you?"

Fernando reached out and cupped her chin in his hand. "Because, querida, when I saw you standing there in that garden, with that beautiful smile on your lips, I knew with a certainty that I'd have to claim them. That I wouldn't rest until I made you mine."

"It was a simple sexual attraction."

"There was nothing simple about it," he said, brushing his lips to hers.

Jess closed her eyes as her heart stilled. She couldn't let herself do this, but she couldn't stop herself either. His masculine scent washed over her as she felt his palm press into the small of her back.

"*Jessica,*" *he said, resting his forehead on hers.* "*When I tell you the truth about this morning, I don't want you to believe that anything last night was a lie.*" *And then to prove it, he kissed her deeply, with a skill and a passion that made her lose grip of her wine, sending the contents of her cup sloshing sideways.*

"*Your sister's riding pants,*" *she said, nearly breathless.*

"*They'll wash,*" *he said, tenderly stroking her thigh.*

"*Fernando,*" *Jess gasped, pulling back.* "*We can't.*"

He studied her a thoughtful moment as she gazed at him wide-eyed.

"*Then we won't,*" *he said with a quick peck on her lips.*

She shivered involuntarily in spite of herself. This man had a way of completely undoing her.

"*We'll have a little something to eat first.*" *He pulled several small bundles from his bag, along with a small knife and a cutting board.*

"*While we talk?*"

"*Of course,*" *he said, handing her a napkin for her slacks.* "*Then afterwards, I'll let you decide.*"

"*Decide what?*"

Fernando shot her a sexy grin as he refilled her wine. "*Whether or not I'm the husband of your dreams.*"

Chapter One

Jess rolled over into a wall of steel. She opened her eyes, encountering a strong, masculine shoulder. Hoofbeats echoed outside to the sound of *ándale, ándale, vámanos*! Her gaze panned the spread of his broad, olive chest, graced with charcoal hair matching the wavy array on his head. Impossibly perfect cheekbones offset a patrician nose. No Renaissance sculptor could have crafted a finer face. Jess's mind whirled, recalling the evening of wild flamenco dancing and sangria. *This slumbering specimen can't be, but he is!*

She gingerly lifted the sheet and peered beneath it with a gasp.

"Good morning, *princesa*," he said, emerald eyes upon her.

Jess pinched the duvet to her chest, her face on fire. "Fernando."

He turned toward her, covers gaping. "I trust you slept well," he said, trailing a finger down her arm. Little shivers raced up her spine, then plummeted in a dead heat toward her tailbone. He brought warm lips to her shoulder, gracing it with a kiss. "I also hope," he said, his Spanish accent trilling, "you meant what you said last night."

Panic tore through her as she desperately tried to recall. Gracefully, he filled in the blank. "That you were happy to be my wife." *Wife? Did he just say wife?*

Fernando tenderly peeled back the duvet, admiring the curve of her hip beneath a satiny sheer nighty. His palm centered on the small of her back as he angled his ruggedly handsome face toward hers. "And you took pains to prove it," he said in a husky rasp, pressing her lower region toward his vivid response.

Jess pushed back with a start and pinched her forearm, certain she would wake up. He lazily pulled himself partially upright on one elbow, resting his head in his hand.

Jess stared, dumbfounded, while Fernando lifted his brow and waited.

"What...is the meaning of this?" she asked, covering herself primly.

"Don Fernando!" a voice called through the screenless window in gruff Castilian. "You still riding this morning?"

Fernando shot Jess a questioning look. She quickly shook her head.

"Not today, Pedrito!" he called back in English. "We're sorry to have troubled you!"

"We?" Jess asked, her voice escaping as a whisper.

"You insisted I take you riding. Don't you recall? It was the second thing you wished to do as my new wife."

Jess felt the heat bolt to her temples and chin. Suddenly, it all came back to her. The late night at the bodega, Fernando's unexpected and utterly passionate kiss, their unanticipated encounter with that Catholic priest... Jess swallowed hard past the burn in her throat.

She'd come to Madrid on an acquisitions merger but had married a matador instead.

Fernando watched as the beautiful woman leapt from the bed, snatching the duvet with her. Honey-blonde hair cascaded past delicate shoulders as she suddenly averted brilliant blue eyes.

"You should cover yourself," she insisted.

"But it seems my new wife has taken the covers."

"And stop saying that!" she cried with an indignant pout.

"What? That you're my wife? I do apologize," he said, sitting upright and scooting to the edge of the bed. "Perhaps it's better if I call you my bride."

Jess instinctively stepped back. "Now, Fernando," she began with a wave of her finger. "You know as well as I do that—if anything happened last night—it wasn't supposed to."

He noticed she was trying not to peek at him but was failing in her efforts. He took this as encouragement to drop his feet to the floor and face her outright, sporting his full glory.

"Is that what you Americans mean by, *Take me back to your bed, you beast. I'm yours?*"

She gasped audibly. "I said that?" she asked with unmasked horror.

Taking pity on the woman, Fernando covered his lap with a feather pillow. "You can look now," he said with a sigh.

She steadied her chin, settling her gaze on the window. "How do I know I can trust you?"

"I guess you don't," he replied. "But I'm inviting you to take the chance."

Slowly, she turned her eyes toward his. They were an amazing shade of blue, aquamarine, really. Fernando felt as if he could swim in them forever. He recalled thinking that yesterday evening, after a few too many pitchers of sangria and a splendidly expensive bottle of cava. Perhaps he'd gotten carried away in asking her to be his bride. But after the flamenco show and the kiss by the fountain, their surprise encounter with his old friend Father Domingo had seemed nothing less than a direct sign from God.

"Where are my clothes?" she asked, color sweeping the bridge of her nose.

Fernando pointed to the armoire beside the door leading to the well-appointed bathroom.

"I suppose the shower's in there?" she asked, angling her head in that direction.

"There are fresh towels on the stand behind the claw-foot tub," he said.

Her cheeks flamed red. Perhaps she did remember everything.

"Fine, thank you," she said hoarsely, sidestepping her way across the floor, the hem of the duvet trailing over inlaid tile.

"Would you like something to eat?" he called after her. "I can have Consuelo bring up breakfast."

She skittered into the bathroom, partially closing the door. "Just coffee!" she called before shutting it with a bang.

Fernando sat upright with a start and tossed aside the pillow.

"Consuelo?" he said into the intercom by the bed, pressing its button.

"*¿Sí, señor?*" a kindly older voice asked from the kitchen.

"*Dos café con leche, por favor.*"

"*Two*, Don Fernando?"

While it had come as surprise, Fernando didn't precisely view his marriage as a mistake. In fact, given the timeline imposed by his grandfather for inheriting his fortune, this little twist of fate just might prove fortuitous.

"*Sí, dos.* And, if you will, place a pretty, fresh rose on the tray. I have something happy to tell you."

Jess let the water run hot, hitting her full in the face. Any second now, she was going to wake up in her apartment in Brooklyn, her best friend Evie calling her on the phone about some recent catastrophe that had occurred... Jess's mind raced, putting pieces of the puzzle together.

Fernando Garcia de la Vega's emerging telecommunications firm had been a long-term associate of her multinational corporation headquartered in New York. While Jess wasn't super tech-savvy, she knew how money worked. Trained in the banking industry, she'd earned her stripes by helping arrange the takeover of United National Savings & Loan's domestic division by InTrust Corp. While she'd really been the second in that job, her magnanimous superior had given her the bulk of the credit. The offer to head up the foreign acquisitions office at Global Financial Telecom had come just two weeks later. She'd accepted the post with a mixture of joy and trepidation. There she was at twenty-eight, and—according to everyone else—finally making her way. Inwardly, she feared she'd bitten off more than she could chew. She'd never handled such a large responsibility alone. What if she made a disaster of it all and failed everybody in the process?

While Global Financial had started as a bank, it quickly expanded into the lucrative computing field, piloting the first purse-size, all-purpose computer. With computing and telecommunications becoming so intricately linked, interest in other types of personal electronic devices followed. So far, Jess had done a reasonable job, impressing her stern, middle-aged boss Madeline with her string of unlikely successes. She didn't know how her mergers had always come through, but it appeared as if she had an invisible good luck charm buried somewhere deep in her pocket. Each time she got assigned to something new, Jess silently feared her luck would run out. Now, it appeared it finally had.

Jess shut off the water and reached for a towel, her gaze panning toward the bedroom. How could she have let herself get swept away? So what if Fernando was gorgeous, intelligent, and had an accent to die for? That was no reason to go shedding her clothes and getting married! Jess cinched the towel around herself, realizing she had that in the wrong order. The marriage part had come before the hopping into bed. But why had she done it? She wasn't that old-fashioned, for heaven's sake. Sleeping with a man after a few too many sangrias and a momentary lapse in judgment was one thing. Saying "I do" under the arch of an orange tree in the courtyard of some small church whose name she couldn't pronounce was something else entirely.

Jess warmed at the memory of Fernando kissing her by the main plaza's fountain, sweetly at first—and then with the passion of a parched man determined to drink her in. Her face flashed hot as she further recalled Fernando's skilled, masculine touch once he'd brought her back to his lair. The ranch was breathtaking in its desolate beauty, rows of olive trees threaded by moonlight, a faraway vineyard trailing over burnt hills.

She hadn't even known he'd come from a family of matadors or had once worked as a bullfighter himself. These were stories he told to few people, he'd assured her with a tender caress before leading her up the stairs. While the townsfolk of La Esperanza del Corazón viewed him as a hero, in Madrid Fernando was just a successful businessman. Neither the family he came from nor the world he'd left behind had any bearing on his corporate potential. So he'd shuttered away his past, vowing to reserve its unveiling only for those special parties with whom he might share a future. He'd led her to his bed then, saying that their impromptu marriage had been a blessing, something he'd never wish undone—no matter how she might think of him tomorrow. And, when he'd offered to show her the scar that tore from his upper left thigh to his navel, she'd found it impossible to say no.

Jess moistened a washcloth from a nearby stand with cool water and pressed it to her chest. Fine trickles slid south, gliding into her cleavage.

Okay, so she'd admit it. Ever since they'd first met six months ago, she'd been reduced to a handful of putty each time he'd given her that deep, expressive look with those impossibly unnerving eyes. Still, she'd steeled herself against him, understanding that when he was being flirty, it was likely in the interest of his own financial gain. That was just what Fernando was: untrustworthy. Which was precisely why she had no reason to trust him now. Fernando was up to something with this marriage bit, and Jess was determined to learn what. But first, she needed to find an Internet connection and research Spanish marriage laws. Surely, things couldn't be as bad as they seemed.

Fernando hummed a love song and strategically angled the tray, rearranging its bud vase for maybe the tenth time. *Ridiculous*, he told himself. It was only a flower. But none could be as sweet as the delicate rose that had opened up for him last night. Fernando would be a liar to say he hadn't wanted her—*ached for her*—for months on end. He'd never seen a face so lovely or known a mind so sharp. Hers was such an intoxicating combination, he might even have married her without the wine.

Though he'd secretly imagined laying her in his bed at least a dozen times, he'd never envisioned the sheer ecstasy of actually being with her. She was so sweet yet tough, like a tiger in the wild. And her kisses were the nearest thing to heaven. If the bright Andalusian sun hadn't awakened him from his slumber, he might have thought he'd fantasized the whole thing. He'd stirred early to find a sleeping angel beside him, then had quickly shut his eyes, lest she evaporate like an enchanted dream. The next thing he knew, she was moving beside him, carefully peering under the sheet to ensure he possessed the correct... accoutrements needed to fulfill his husbandly duties. Fernando sighed, thinking he'd be glad to perform those again and at any time his willing wife was ready.

He stared toward the bathroom, noting the shower had stopped. This might not be the most standard way to begin a union, but it certainly couldn't be the worst. Fernando was sure that Jessica would agree—once she got over the shock.

Jess exited the bathroom with a combative air and made a beeline for the armoire.

"Coffee this morning?" he asked, smiling sweetly over the rim of a cup. He extended it in her direction with the calm demeanor of a waiter at an upscale restaurant. She noted his lower region was still covered by a large feather pillow, the musculature of his tanned upper thighs exposed to the morning breeze fluttering in through the window. His toned olive chest sported richly dark hair which tapered in perfect symmetry down the line of his taut abs and plummeted toward the breakfast tray balanced on his lap.

She hesitated a moment, then decided she'd think better after the java. "Fernando," she said, cinching the oversized towel around her and cautiously inching forward. "You and I have something to discuss."

He handed her the coffee, then nonchalantly dipped a bit of pastry in his own cup. "I never discuss business before breakfast," he said, slurping loudly. "Mmm. This *pan dulce* is delicious. You ought to try it."

"I'm not hungry," she said, steadying the cup in her hands.

"Ah yes, that's right," he replied with a knowing wave of his finger. "Fairly well satisfied last night. Eh?"

Jess felt her face flash hot as his impish green eyes danced with mirth. "I don't find any of this very amusing."

"I'm sorry, Jessica," he said sadly. "I suppose I was a fool, hoping that you'd be just as excited about this as I."

She took a slow sip of coffee, studying him all the while. "You claim to be a fool, Fernando. But you're certainly not fooling me."

He raised his brow, perplexed.

"Come on," she said. "Give. What's in this for you?"

"My new wife has cut me to the quick," he said, bringing a hand to his chest.

"Argh!" She spun toward the armoire, clumsily setting down her cup down on a nearby stand. Porcelain clattered against itself with the effort.

"You're getting too upset about this," he said.

"I...don't...think...so," she said as she furiously tugged her clothes from huge wooden hangers, then strode toward the bathroom.

"*Querida*," Fernando said softly, "please wait."

She stopped walking, her pulse pounding. It picked up as she felt him behind her, his warmth drawing near. Instinct said that Fernando hadn't carried the pillow—or anything else—with him. "Perhaps it was...impetuous, unexpected," he said, palms pressed to her bare upper arms. Goose bumps rose on her flesh as the heat of his breath warmed her neck. "But you can't completely believe it was wrong."

But it was wrong, worse than wrong. Marrying Fernando had to be the most terrible decision she'd ever made!

"I have a boyfriend," she said, the lie escaping as a whisper.

"What a shame." Palms slid down her arms as Fernando brought his lips to her shoulder. "How do you think he'll take the news?"

Jess gasped, fighting her automatic feminine response. Nipples hardened beneath terrycloth, and she ached to turn toward him. Being made love to by a strong, confident man like Fernando was nothing short of heaven. The truth was that she and Allen had broken up weeks ago, and the physical relationship they'd shared hadn't even come close. Still, the illusion of another man was good, maybe the best thing she had at the moment. Until her head cleared, Jess needed every ounce of ammunition against Fernando's manly advances that she could muster.

"He'll be outraged," she said, pulling her mound of clothing in tighter.

"He must love you desperately."

Jess pursed her lips, fighting the fire in her eyes. The fact was, she didn't know whether Allen had loved her or not. Just as with her past two boyfriends, he'd never broached the topic—and she'd never yearned to discuss it.

"I don't do love," she said hoarsely, making an effort to step away.

Fernando tightened his grip and spun her toward him. "Everybody *does* love," he said with an earnest look. "Sooner or later."

Jess blinked back the moisture in her eyes. "Not this girl."

Fernando released her, his brow creasing. He'd never seen a woman at once so fragile and strong. There was a sorrow in her eyes that made him want to weep for, and with, her. He wondered how long she'd contained it, keeping that sadness to herself.

"I'll just be a minute," she said, turning away.

Fernando watched her leave, thinking this presented more of a challenge than he'd imagined. Then again, if ever there was a man who knew how to rise to the occasion, it was him.

"Take all the time that you need," he said as she exited the room.

Jessica emerged fully dressed ten minutes later. "As soon as we return to Madrid," she said, "we're getting this thing annulled."

She was beautiful today, smartly polished in a short white dress. He'd be proud to introduce her, if only she'd trade that frown on her lips for one of those winning smiles.

"Annulled?" Fernando questioned, glancing sideways as he straightened the collar of his polo shirt in the mirror. "Don't you think that's a little rash?"

"No, Fernando. Rash is getting married to a business colleague after too much sangria. Rash is *not* doing the sensible thing the next morning."

Jess didn't know how she'd let herself get talked into it, but she had. Right down to signing that statement of Proof of Freedom to Marry, endorsed by Father Domingo's brother-in-law, the retired American Consul, whose powers of persuasion were still apparently in force.

"But we weren't married in Madrid," he noted astutely.

Jess considered this a moment, realizing he was right. The marriage had to be annulled right here. But first, she needed to learn precisely where that was. "Where are we?"

"In La Esperanza del Corazón, remember? Place of my birth."

Yes, it all came stampeding back to her, like a trillion *toros* on the run. "Of course I recall."

"Everything...?" he asked, suggestively lifting an eyebrow.

Jess shook her head in agitation. She was not going to let him do this, have her remembering all the *wrong* things. "I was tipsy…animated, okay? Foolishly and hopelessly in love with life!"

He beheld her wistfully. "Yes, it was lovely."

Jess fought for the words. "It was reckless," she countered. "That woman you were with last night wasn't me."

"No? Who was it?"

"Someone else." She huffed, trying to imagine how she'd explain this to her mother. Jess had never gotten so much as a B on a report card. Now here she was, failing life. "My evil twin."

He laughed out loud. "You're a Gemini?"

"What?"

"The zodiac sign."

She was puzzled by this turn in the conversation.

"What do constellations have to do with anything?"

"Perhaps we're written in the stars," he said, a sly smile on his lips.

Jess pressed her palms to her temples, thinking hard. Before she told her mother, she'd call Evie; that was what she'd do. Evie would help her straighten things out. If Jess could fix things fast, maybe her mom wouldn't even have to know.

"I'm a Taurus, if it matters."

"I might have guessed."

"What's that's supposed to mean?"

"The Taurus and the toreador? And you tell me there's no fate?"

She set her jaw, her eyes boring into his. "Fernando Garcia de la Vega, I want you to show me to an Internet connection this minute!"

"That might be a bit complicated. You see, out here *en el campo*, we have limited..." His voice fell off as he took in her increasingly enraged form. It was one thing to lightheartedly provoke someone. But at this very moment, Fernando sensed he was putting himself in mortal danger. "Okay, all right," he said, flagging a hand in her direction. "I can see when I'm not wanted."

His expression took a downcast turn that almost made her feel sorry for him. The truth was, Jess had wanted him, *wanted him in the worst way*, which was precisely what had gotten her into this mess! She pulled her cell from her purse and checked it for the tenth time this morning. She still wasn't picking up service. Just how far from civilization were they?

Fernando gestured grandly toward the door that led downstairs. He unlocked it, then held it open. "Fair's fair, Jessica. After all, no one's holding you prisoner in an ivory tower. So, here's what we'll do. You and I will have a civilized talk about everything that happened last night. Then, if you're still determined to get out of this marriage, I won't stop you. I'm far too proud a man to hold a woman against her will."

Jess's heart skipped a beat as something raw and unanticipated burned inside her. She couldn't say whether it was relief she felt or something more akin to disappointment. Why, oh why did his admission that he was fine in letting her go resonate with something so utterly painful in her core?

Jess shook off the odd déjà vu and met his gaze, his green eyes playing the soft serenade of a Spanish guitar. Jess caught her breath, lost for a moment in their music.

"I also believe," he said slowly, "that sometimes things happen for a reason. And often that reason is far too grand for us to originally understand."

But Jess didn't want to think about reasons or fate or star-crossed lovers—or any of that other nonsense Evie so ardently believed in but that she'd never been able to wrap her own head around. Jess was a practical person who saw the world for what it was. The fact that she'd long ago stopped believing in fairy tales had only worked to her benefit.

"The only thing I need to understand," she said, "is why you persist in saying this…accident of nature…was somehow preordained. "

He massaged his temples, apparently growing exasperated. "I already said I'll explain everything."

"Good," she said, stepping past him. "At last, you're talking sensibly."

Jess hurried down the stairs, desperate to get away. He smelled of sandalwood soap and lime, and the aroma awakened her memory of his showering kisses last night. The sooner she got herself out of this mistake of an arrangement, the better. And it better be before nightfall, lest she find herself tempted to leap back into that manly matador's bed.

"I've never been accused of being unreasonable," he said, trailing after her. "But I am known for keeping my commitments."

Jess halted in her tracks, fearing this was going somewhere. Somewhere that was going to land dangerously close to further confounding her emotions.

He captured her in his gaze, stilling her heart for a fraction of a second. Somehow, when he looked at her, it was as if he could see into her depths and behold her every weakness. And yet, his gaze soothed her, smoothing old hurts in tender ways. Warmth surged in her cheeks as he descended the steps two at a time, then gently cupped her face in his hands.

"And I *always* honor my commitments," he said, his voice a husky rasp.

Her pulse beat wildly, and for a second, she feared he would kiss her. Next, she was terribly afraid he might not.

"Most especially," he continued with an enigmatic smile, "to my mother."

End of sample from How to Marry a Matador.